STO

ACPL IT

Y0-BVP-899
DISCARDED

TEEN VIOLENCE

by Susan S. Lang

Revised Edition

FRANKLIN WATTS
NEW YORK/CHICAGO/LONDON/TORONTO/SYDNEY

Photographs copyright ©: Wide World Photos: pp. 10, 119; Stock Montage, Chicago: p. 15; The New York Historical Society: p. 17; Photo Researchers, Inc.: pp. 33 (Jan Haluska), 38 (Steve Kagan), 53 bottom, 76, 79 (all Richard Hutchings), 109 (Blair Seitz), 138 (David M. Grossman); Impact Visuals: p. 53 top (Katherine McGlynn), 101 (Teun Voeten), 153 (Amy Zuckerman); Monkmeyer Press Photo: pp. 59 (Irene Bayer), 127 (Nancy Hayes); Gamma-Liaison: pp. 62, 143 (both Stephen Ferry), 70 (Yvonne Hemsey), 95 (Claudio Edinger); UPI/Bettmann Newsphotos: p. 84; The New York Post/Ralph Ginzburg: p. 93.

Library of Congress Cataloging-in-Publication Data

Lang, Susan S.
Teen violence / by Susan S. Lang.—Rev. ed.
p.   cm.
Includes bibliographical references and index.
ISBN 0-531-11202-0
1. Juvenile delinquency—United States—Juvenile literature.
2. Violence—United States—Juvenile literature.
3. Juvenile delinquency—United States—Prevention—Juvenile literature.
[1. Juvenile delinquency. 2. Violence.] I. Title.
HV9104.L32   1994
364.3'6'0973—dc20   94-34475 CIP AC

CONTENTS

For Julia;
may her generation be more at peace

ACKNOWLEDGMENTS

A thank-you to Susan Terkel for getting me involved in writing books for young adults. A most special thanks to my husband, Tom Schneider, for his endless patience, thoughtful input, and loving support.

TEEN VIOLENCE

1

TRUE STORIES

People have always accused kids of getting away with murder. Now that is all too literally true. Across the U.S., a pattern of crime has emerged that is both perplexing and appalling. Many youngsters appear to be robbing and raping, maiming and murdering as casually as they go to a movie or join a pickup baseball game. A new remorseless, mutant juvenile seems to have been born, and there is no more terrifying figure in America today.[1]
—Time magazine

What began playfully as a dreamy night of kissing for seventeen-year-old Michelle Marie Hayes turned into a nightmare of death.

It was a warm night in July 1985 in Mentor, Ohio, a small town near Cleveland. Scott Grant, eighteen, a good-looking high school student with scraggly bleached-blond hair, had made plans for Michelle to come over to his friend's house, where he was staying.

Scott was "a druggy type" and loved to brag to other kids about the fights he got into. He sometimes got into trouble with teachers and even occasionally with the police, but people in his town described him as a smart kid and pretty easygoing. Most people liked him.

Scott told his friend, Steve Cohen, a rugged-looking sixteen-year-old with a drug history, that Michelle was going to come over. The boys listened to some music before she arrived. Scott then describes what happened next.

> Steve greeted Michelle at the utility window when she arrived. . . . I noticed her trying to hit on me. I could tell Steve got jealous because he stormed upstairs. Then, Michelle and I were talking for a while and then we started kissing. We gradually worked our way to Steve's bed. . . .
>
> Steve came downstairs and was watching us. I could tell Michelle got upset because she was staring at him and asked him to leave and he wouldn't. Then she yelled at me to stop what I was doing and then kept bitching at me, saying, "Stop, please, no. . . ."[2]

The evening of sex continued to turn darker. As Scott told police:

> I smacked her with a right across the cheek so she would shut up because she was going to wake the house up. Then she started calling me names like bastard and hitting me, so I punched her in the throat so she would shut up. I learned Tae Kwan Do from a friend, and he said that makes people stop talking. Michelle started choking and twitching after that, and I didn't know what to do. . . .[3]

Michelle stopped talking, all right—the two boys realized she was dead. No one knows what these boys were thinking when they decided to cut her legs off with a handsaw. Then they tossed her body into a berry patch behind Steve's house.

"We talked and told each other not to say anything to anybody. Then we went back to Steven's house and went to bed."[4]

The boys ended up going to prison. What frightened their community most was that Steve and Scott had seemed like ordinary kids before they killed and butchered Michelle for no apparent reason. Worse yet, nationwide their senseless crime did not stand alone; it was just one of a host of others in which teens had shot, stabbed, clubbed, and strangled people to death.

Glen Ridge High is nestled in a fancy New Jersey suburb near Manhattan. The two most popular boys in the senior class were twins Kevin and Kyle Scherzer. They were the football co-captains, "calendar handsome, never at a loss for a date."[5] One grim March day, the boys were throwing a ball near their home with some friends, other baseball and football stars from Glen Ridge High. The boys caught sight of a local seventeen-year-old girl whom many of them had known since first grade.

"We want to talk to you," one boy yelled out to her. "We won't hurt you."[6]

The boys coaxed the girl down to the twins' half-finished basement where they often pumped iron. The girl was mildly retarded and yearned for approval from these popular and good-looking boys. She trusted these kids, she later told police, so she went downstairs. Thirteen boys followed, including the high school's most liked, most handsome star athletes.

Then these "good kids" brutally assaulted her, forcing broomsticks and other objects into her vagina. One of the boys, the son of a local police lieutenant, was directly responsible for forcing a small-scale baseball bat into the girl. At least six of the others stood around watching.

News of the assault buzzed around study halls and the locker room for months. The boys bragged about it, cocky that they had gotten away with it. Other kids in the school reported that these "jocks" also got away with stealing cars and drunk driving. "Some kids said jocks got away with so much, they didn't know wrong from right anymore,"[7] wrote journalist Peter Wilkinson.

After three months of gossip, bragging, and cover-up, some of the boys were finally arrested. But as of this writing, the legal proceedings are crawling at a snail's pace. Whether any of the boys will be convicted or go to jail remains to be seen.

Wednesday, April 19, 1989, was a warm, clear, early-spring night in Central Park in New York City. The silver light of an almost full moon lit the faces of groups of teenage boys. Thirty to forty youths, ages thirteen to seventeen, were wandering through the park. Although one had mentioned earlier in the day that he wanted to go "wilding" that night, most of the boys were just going along with the crowd. But what started as a group of frisky youths swiftly changed into a pack of rampaging teenage thugs.

Some were "good kids" from caring families. Others had gotten into trouble at school.

That April night, they all got into trouble—deep trouble. The boys formed savage roaming packs, attacking "joggers and bicyclists in the park for fun."[8] By 10 P.M., they had assaulted eight people at random, including an old Hispanic man, whom they punched and kicked into unconsciousness.

Then they came upon a twenty-nine-year-old woman, an investment banker who was jogging by a grove of sycamore trees.

The teenage "wolf pack" chased the young woman

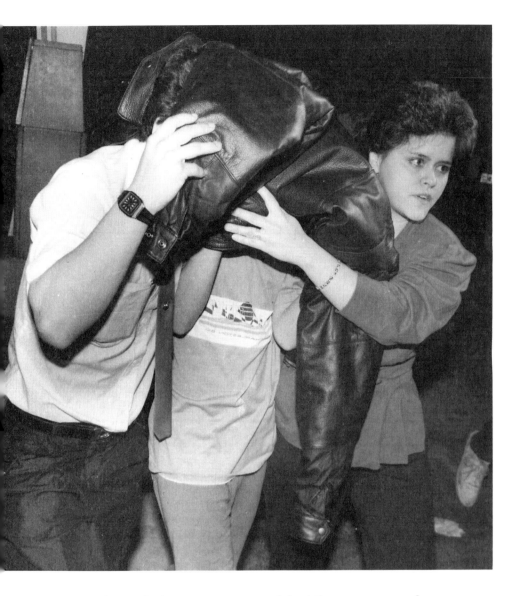

Are today's teenagers more violent than young people in the past? The two teenagers shown here have just been charged with being part of a group of seventeen youths who allegedly beat two groundskeepers with golf clubs in a park in New York City.

down a gully, tackled her, "hacked her skull and thighs with a knife, [and] punched her face with a brick."[9] Why? "Because it was fun."[10] After she stopped yelling and her eyes closed, the boys used her bloody sweatshirt to tie her hands up, and then at least seven of them raped her. They left her for dead in the cool mud.

By the time the woman was found three hours later, she had lost three-quarters of her blood and had lapsed into a coma. Doctors expected her to die. Her head was so coated in the cold mud, though, that the swelling of her brain was controlled. After two weeks in a coma and seven months in the hospital, she was released. Doctors called her recovery a miracle.

Before that night, these boys were known as basically good kids, from families whose parents worked hard and cared a lot about their children. Four of the boys lived in apartment buildings with doormen or security guards; one played the tuba and was a talented artist; another received a daily four-dollar allowance. The kids "were described variously as shy or loners or good listeners, children of strict parents."[11]

After their arrest, one prosecutor told the court that the boys were joking, laughing, and carrying on in the precinct house, not showing any remorse or concern for their victim. They whistled at a policewoman and sang the rap song "Wild Thing" in the holding pen. The gang did what they did, one told the police, because "it was something to do."[12] Another reported that after the attack, the boys "were exuberant—laughing and acting stupid, leaping and cavorting in the air."[13]

What is happening to some of today's teenagers? Are the times different now? Are teenagers more violent than they used to be? Are these isolated stories or manifestations of a significant social problem that too many people ignore? Why are some kids stabbing, shooting, and attacking each other and innocent victims? What can be done about it?

2

OUR VIOLENT SOCIETY

Violence has been far more intrinsic to our past than we would like to think . . . . The patriot, the humanitarian, the nationalist, the pioneers, the landholder, the farmer, and the laborer, have used violence as the means to a higher end . . . . So great has been our involvement with both negative and positive violence over the long sweep of our history that violence has truly become a part of our unacknowledged (or underground) value structure.[1]

—*1969 National Commission on the Causes and Prevention of Violence*

The United State of America, perhaps the greatest democracy in the history of the world, is also the most violent industrialized society in the world today. In fact, we are a nation born out of violence.

WHAT IS VIOLENCE?

Violence is the threat or use of force that injures or intimidates a person (makes one feel afraid) or damages property. The major kinds of violent crimes against people include:

- Assault: threatening to attack, trying to attack, or actually attacking someone else with or without a weapon

- Aggravated assault: attacking someone so badly that it hurts them seriously, or threatening or trying to attack someone with a weapon in order to kill or hurt them badly
- Battery: using physical force or violence against another person
- Rape: trying to or succeeding in having sex with someone without his or her consent by using force or the threat of force
- Robbery: stealing directly from a person by force or by threatening to use force, with or without a weapon
- Homicide: killing another person[2]

OUR VIOLENT HISTORY

Most historians would agree that "throughout its short history, there has been a huge amount of violence in the United States, much of it associated with glory and the construction of a 'better' America. . . . In fact, violence is traditional,"[3] writes forensic psychiatrist (a doctor who studies the criminal mind) John Gunn.

One of the primary forces motivating the early European explorers who opened the New World in the sixteenth and seventeenth centuries was the search for riches to finance the almost constant wars in Europe.

The New World conjured up glittering visions of endless opportunities. For peasants in Europe in the 1500s, a life of poverty and misery was cast at birth. For people who followed unpopular religions, life was dangerous, as enemies chased them out of homes and jobs, and sometimes out of the country. The long and dangerous trip to the New World seemed worth the risk, the only hope to change an otherwise bleak future.

But as immigrants began to pour in, their dreams were quickly shattered. To expand their settlements, colonists first had to wage bloody battles to push Indian tribes off their lands. The Indian Removal Bill, one of the darkest chapters in U.S. history, essentially ordered the killing of Indians and/or their forcible relocation to barren lands, lands incapable of sustaining cultural and family traditions.

But violence also erupted continually among the settlers themselves. From its very inception, the New World was a "nation of immigrants." Although those who took the chance left their homes seeking a shining torch of freedom, the tragic truth is that minority ethnic groups have always been the source of scorn and victims of violence in the United States. They have been flushed out, terrorized, shot, or lynched, and they've had their homes trashed and burned to the ground.

Violence has always been the way that "the haves"—those with power, money, and resources—have threatened those without, the "have-nots." Typically, the haves feel threatened by the have-nots, fearful that the latter will gain power and valued resources. Although the history of the United States is painted with compassion, disturbing violent streaks stain it throughout.

Settlers found themselves under the tyranny of church leaders who were also the government leaders. These local theocracies (governments run by church leaders) often resorted to violence to scare off settlers who worshiped God differently or to coerce them into being more like them.

Then the victims of violence were the Indians and later the blacks, chained and dragged from their African homelands. Later victims included Catholics, Irish, Jews and eastern Europeans, Chinese, and today, Caribbean blacks, Southeast Asians, and other ethnic minorities.

This country's independence was gained only after a bloody revolution in 1776. When the American Constitution was drawn up, the seeds for a permanent underclass were planted: Each black slave was to be counted as only three-fifths of a white man for purposes of representation in Congress.

The history of the United States is rife with
incidents of violence against individuals and
groups. Numerous conflicts with Indians took
place during our early frontier days.

After slavery became a Southern institution, bitter battles raged between slave owners and abolitionists, who wanted to outlaw slavery. The conflicts led to the devastating Civil War of the early 1860s, which tore the country into shreds. In many areas of the United States, wounds still sting.

Immediately after the Civil War, resentments, anxiety, and fear abounded in the war-torn South because a way of life was being forced to change. Many whites feared the changes Reconstruction would bring. In this climate, the Ku Klux Klan was born. Disguised in long, white hooded robes, white men lynched, beat, and terrorized blacks and then later Jews and Catholics. Today, the Klan still carries its banner of bigotry and hate and has added other minorities to its hit list.

But starting well before the Civil War, throughout the 1700s and 1800s, pioneers were forever pushing the frontier westward, fulfilling the national goal of Manifest Destiny. With so much land and so few living on it, people often took the law and justice into their own hands. Vigilantes determined "on the spot" justice, with suspected criminals often punished at the wrong end of a pistol or a rope.

By the late 1800s, as immigrants began to arrive in tidal waves, conflicts erupted constantly among ethnic and racial groups. Even today, violence is waged by those who feel threatened by people who are different. Such xenophobia (fear of those who are different) daily threatens the well-being of blacks, Jews, Asians, Hispanics, and other minorities.

As industry boomed in the late 1800s, cities swelled and the rich hired the poor to work the factories, mines, railroads, and seaports. The gap between the rich and poor grew, and the life of the working masses became ever more miserable. As labor tried to organize to improve its working conditions, disputes between labor and management frequently flared up into violence.

Above: **The massacre of Chinese in Rock Spring, Wyoming, during the late 1800s is another example of violence against minorities. The homes of the Chinese were set on fire and the people shot as they tried to flee.**

Right:
The violence against blacks in the United States has been well documented. This riot took place in New Orleans in 1866.

At the same time, corruption in cities grew and organized crime was born. Such groups as the Mafia used violence to gain control of businesses, industries, and communities.

The 1900s have been marked by minorities' being squeezed into urban ghettos, economically forced into unsafe, dirty, and overcrowded dwellings. Abroad, the nation participated in violent wars around the world. At home, the black underclass, growing ever more frustrated by its plight, was pushed to violence in its battle for civil rights.

More recently, street crime has soared as drugs and guns saturate the land. Many youths who face few job options have turned to drugs as a way to escape the poverty, despair, and broken dreams of ghetto life and a means to earn a living.

Anyone watching television or reading newspapers confronts violence daily. We have become, to a large extent, a nation used to violence in our daily lives.

OUR VIOLENT SOCIETY

Violence is a fact of life in America today. Some grim yet typical examples:

- In upstate New York, a family of four was found dead three days before Christmas morning. The victims—the parents, a fifteen-year-old girl who played on the high school tennis team, and an eleven-year-old Boy Scout—had been tied up, shot in the head, doused with gasoline, and set on fire. The motive: robbery and the elimination of its witnesses.
- In Los Angeles, fifty-seven-year-old Charles Padilla took his two grandchildren for a ride in his car to buy film. He was cut off by a car with two men in it. One of the men walked up to Padilla's car and asked, "What's your problem?" Padilla tried to roll his window up, but the stranger pulled out a gun and shot him in the back of the head.

- In Edmund, Oklahoma, Patrick Henry Sherrill was angry because he lost his job at the post office. Shortly afterward he walked into the post office and shot twenty people, killing fourteen.
- In Washington, D.C., fifteen-year-old Sean Smith was a hardworking teen at the local Athlete's Foot store. When someone stole his new hundred-dollar red ski parka, he got into an argument with a man, who pulled a gun and shot him dead.
- In Norwalk, Connecticut, a former airline pilot was sentenced to fifty years in prison for killing his wife. He was reported to have cut her body up with a chain saw and then shredded it piece by piece in a wood chipper. His sister complained that the man showed no remorse.

Horrible crimes like these occur everyday, everywhere—in cities, suburbs, and the countryside. "The level of violent crime in the United States remains astronomical—much higher than in other industrialized democratic nations,"[4] reports Lynn A. Curtis, a former member of the National Commission on the Causes and Prevention of Violence and codirector of the Crimes of Violence Task Force.

By 1994, crime emerged in numerous polls as the top concern among Americans. And for good reason. Violent crime is ripping apart the fabric of our society.[5] Although it had leveled off in the early 1980s, since the mid-1980s, it has been on the increase. Between 1960 and 1992, the number of reported violent crimes jumped 371 percent,[6] to an estimated 1.8 million.[7] Between 1982 and 1992, the rate of violent crimes rose by one-third, from 562 violent crimes per 100,000 persons in 1982 to 758 in 1992.[8] The actual rate of violent crime, however, is estimated to be more than three times the reported rate. This means there were about 6 million[9] violent crimes committed in 1992.

In the mid-1970s more than 20,000 homicides were

reported each year in the U.S.; in 1980 the figure grew to 23,040, and by 1992 to 23,760.[10] Although the statistics have not yet been updated, experts fear that 1993 might set yet a new record.

Unfortunately, violent crime is spreading like a vile cancer from the poorest inner cities into the suburbs and rural areas. Smaller cities such as Omaha, New Orleans, and New Haven, as well as smaller towns, must cope with rising levels of crime. As teens around the country have greater access to guns, disputes over girls' jackets, and dirty looks are resolved with a gun instead of a fist.

"Years ago, guys would duke it out with their fists. Now they whip out their Magnum and start firing,"[11] says a Milwaukee police lieutenant.

A district attorney in Monroe County, New York, agrees: "Over the past few years there has been a great increase in the level of violence against victims. There's a general viciousness on the part of the defendants."[12]

"There's more of a lawless attitude among certain parts of our society, less concern for human life, more hostility,"[13] reports an FBI supervisor in Rochester, New York.

Crimes are not only more grisly but more senseless, with strangers brutalizing strangers, sometimes in a robbery but sometimes just for fun, and young thugs shooting blindly from cars in record numbers of drive-by shootings. These new trends are among the most frightening in the crime-wave picture.

Yet the vast majority of such criminals never go to jail. For every 100 violent crimes in this nation, only forty-seven are reported to the police, and only twenty-two suspects are arrested. Eleven are convicted, but only two go to prison.

WHAT DOES THIS VIOLENCE MEAN?

Violence seems to lurk everywhere we look. "It has come to be that we expect violence . . . in some form

every day. Each shocking scene inures us, hardens us.
. . . We casually dismiss daily disasters affecting other
people as routine,"[14] says Robert Clarke, Ph.D., author
of *Deadly Force, The Lure of Violence.*

But for the 6.6 million Americans who fall victim to
violent crime every year,[15] their lives are shattered.
Those who survive the violence carry emotional scars
that hurt for years. Fear, anger, and grief pervade their
lives. Despair, nightmares, guilt, shame, feelings of loss
of control and of vulnerability mark their days and
nights.

Violent crime also affects the close friends and family
members of every victim. The senseless loss of a
twelve-year-old to violence haunts family, friends, and
a community for years.

WHO COMMITS THE VIOLENCE?

Since minorities tend to populate inner-city ghettos and
compose a much larger proportion of the lower socioeconomic levels, a much higher proportion of violent
crimes are committed by minorities and against minorities.

About 90 to 95 percent of those arrested for violent
crimes are either unemployed, underemployed, or living below the poverty level. Blacks make up about 12.1
percent of the American population, but account for
more than half of the arrests for murder, rape, and nonnegligent manslaughter, five times the rate for whites.[16]
All told, more than half the violent crimes in America
are attributed to minorities attacking minorities, with
the exception of robbery, whose victims are just as
likely to be white.[17]

Arrest rates, however, are not an accurate reflection
of the crime rate among races. Although police report
much higher arrest rates for blacks proportionate to
their representation in the population, studies reveal
that these arrests significantly underestimate crimes

committed by whites who are never caught.[18] In 1987, for example, blacks were arrested at three times the rate of whites for aggravated assault, yet the National Crime Survey, based on victim interviews, found that whites attack proportionately just as often.[19]

Further, when poverty is controlled for in studies looking at race and homicide, the racial differences pretty much wash out. In other words, homicide isn't so much linked to race as it is to economic differences: The deprived commit and are victims of more violent crime than are the comfortable.[20]

Also, minorities account for more violent crimes because the police patrol their neighborhoods much more rigorously than white areas and are more alert to minority crime. Also, whites are typically given the benefit of the doubt more often.

Simply, the "criminal justice system, like other sectors of society, discriminates against minorities and the poor,"[21] says Marvin E. Wolfgang, a well-known criminologist at the Center for the Interdisciplinary Study of Criminal Violence and a leading delinquency and criminal-violence researcher. Despite all the gains in civil rights, our society is still racist, a fact few want to believe yet few can deny.

Many more violent crimes are committed by teenagers than any other age group. The next chapter will explore teen violence and who these kids are.

Societies that tolerate prejudice, bigotry, and racism are societies that breed crime. Fear, anger, confusion, and no hope for a better future also contribute to crime, particularly increasingly violent and wanton crime. The next chapter will explore why teenagers commit more violent crimes than any other age group.

3

A VIOLENT SOCIETY BREEDS VIOLENT CHILDREN

There are kids out there who would love to put on their camouflage and hold a knife in their mouth and go out and slit someone's throat. . . . You see them on their way to school with books in one hand and an ice cream cone in another, and you would never know it.[1]

—*An Ohio police sergeant*

- A fifteen-year-old boy refused to give another boy a "high five," a slapping of hands in camaraderie. The snub cost him his life: he was shot dead soon afterward.

- A fourteen-year-old boy was visiting a girl when her mother walked in. The mother started arguing with the boy. Frustrated, he pulled out a gun. When the mother reached for it, he shot her; when she hit the floor, he shot her again in the heart. The girl started screaming and hitting the boy, so he turned the gun on her and shot her in the face.

- A ten-year-old boy stabbed and beat to death a neighbor, a 101-year-old woman. Sent to a state youth facility, the boy will be set free when he turns twenty-one. He will be on the street again until he commits another crime, which according to statistics, he probably will. Both his parents are themselves ex-convicts.
- As a couple napped on a bench in a park in Brooklyn, five teenagers doused them with rubbing alcohol and set them on fire.
- In Warren, Ohio, a seventeen- and an eighteen-year-old boy raped and beat a twelve-year-old Boy Scout to death. The details of the murder were so grisly and shocking that the local newspaper consistently put warnings at the head of its stories about the murder.
- A nine-year-old boy in Pennsylvania, a Cub Scout and honor student with no history of problems, allegedly unlocked his father's gun cabinet, loaded a gun, removed a screen from his family's second-story window, and shot a seven-year-old girl fatally in the back as she whizzed by on a snowmobile. The reason? Some say it was because she bragged about being better at Nintendo.

As blood from violence stains the American way of life, it splatters all over America's youths. Not only have teenagers become more violent, but children as young as seven and eight years old are also committing more violence and with even greater brutality.

Teen crime seems on the rise, although it's hard to know for sure because police records on minors are not public and statistics today are collected differently than in the past. Yet, teen violence is so serious in America that former U.S. Surgeon General C. Everett Koop has called it "an extensive and chronic epidemic in American society."[2]

TEEN CRIME

Attorney General Janet Reno declared in 1993 that teen violence was the greatest single crime problem in America. Teenagers are the most likely age group to commit crimes: sixteen-year-olds commit more crimes against property than any other age group; eighteen-year-olds commit the most violent crimes.[3]

Just as rates for violence are climbing again throughout society, rates for teen and child violence are climbing steadily, too. In 1947, only 16 percent of the arrests in this country involved persons twenty-one years of age or younger; by 1976, that percentage soared to 60 percent.[4] Between 1965 and 1985, violent crimes by those eighteen and younger more than doubled.[5]

From 1987 to 1991, youth arrests for violent crimes jumped yet another 50 percent, almost twice that for people over 18, though the teen population has remained fairly constant or declined. "Most alarming, juvenile arrests for murder increased by 85 percent, compared with 21 percent for those age 18 and over," say the authors of a July 1993 report of the Office of Juvenile Justice and Delinquency Prevention.[6]

In 1985, the school-age population began to climb again after a fifteen-year decline; it's expected to peak around the year 2000. In the meantime, teen crime continues to climb, too.[7] The FBI reports that between 1983 and 1987, for youths aged eighteen and younger, total arrests jumped 22 percent; arrests for aggravated assault, almost 19 percent; for rape, almost 15 percent.[8] According to the author of the recent book *Kids Who Kill*, juvenile homicides have soared five times faster in the last five years of the 1980s than homicides committed by adults.[9]

In 1988, almost 1.6 million teens were arrested, including 69,000 for violent crimes.[10] By 1990, 2.2 million teens under age 18 were arrested, of which 114,000 were for violent crimes, the highest figure in more than 25 years.[11]

The year 1991 also saw a high rate of children and teens arrested for violent crimes: 3,400 were arrested for murder, 6,300 for forcible rape, 44,500 for robbery, and 68,700 for aggravated assault. Of all the violent crime arrests in 1991, juveniles between 10 and 17 years of age were apprehended for 17 percent.[12]

Teen violence is but a reflection of society's violence. Sociologist Murray Straus of the University of New Hampshire has found that as adults commit more murders, teenagers commit more murders. But a frightening new trend has emerged: teens are responsible for an ever increasing proportion of murders and other violent crimes.

WHO ARE THE VIOLENT TEENS?

About three-quarters of the youths arrested in 1990 were male; about one-quarter, female.[13] And although a vast majority of violent teenagers has always been male, females are catching up faster than ever. In Massachusetts, for example, 15 percent of the convictions that teen girls received in 1987 were for violent crimes; by 1992, that rate had more than tripled: 38 percent of the convictions for girls were for violent crimes largely because more and more girls were joining gangs.[14] Nevertheless, according to FBI statistics, more than 90 percent of the teens arrested for murder, nonnegligent manslaughter, weapons law violations, sex offenses, robbery and burglary are males.

Overall, "The teen crime wave flows across all races, classes and life-styles,"[15] reports *Time.* Interestingly, although delinquency rates between white and nonwhite teen boys are about the same, nonwhites get caught much more often. "Put simply, nonwhites and low-class persons are not really more delinquent but are just more likely to be arrested,"[16] says Marvin E. Wolfgang of the Center for the Interdisciplinary Study of Criminal

Violence and a researcher in delinquency and criminal violence. In fact, between 1977 and 1982, black teens accounted for more than half the arrests of teens for violent crimes, with forty-four times more black teens in jail than white teens.[17]

Perhaps most ominous, however, is that recent reports have revealed that one out of four college-age black men is in prison or on probation—more than are in college.[18]

Basically, there are two types of violent teenagers. One is the "good" kid who "out of the blue" commits a very violent crime, usually against a family member or friend. Rather than coming from a caring, nurturing family with positive role models, these children typically have a history of being rejected and abused. Over the years, their anger and hostility builds up, until one day rage overcomes them, hurling them out of control and into violence.

A model youth can become a murderer. He may be so out of control as to knife his victim again and again. Typically, after his violent rage, the killer becomes passive again.[19]

The second type of violent youth is a "career offender"—typically male, black, and poor—who regularly breaks the law and occasionally is violent. Rather than quietly accepting their fate until they explode, these kids tend to lash out violently when frustrated. They have little control over anger, filled with feelings of suspicion, fear, and rage, and often carry a knife or gun.

"This youth frequently comes from a subculture of violence, and he sees violence as a necessary part of the struggle for survival,"[20] says sociologist Clemens Bartollas, a former director of a maximum-security youth facility. There is not a particular subgroup that accounts for most of the violence in this group; rather, these delinquent boys become violent periodically and rather randomly.

Most violent criminals begin their lawless careers while teenagers and young adults[21] and exhibit their violent streaks by age ten if boys and by age thirteen if girls.[22]

Many studies about violent criminals in the United States have been conducted. When pieced together, a profile of the "typical" violent criminal emerges:

> He is young—in his late teens or early twenties. He is unmarried and has a sorry work record. If he does not have a serious heroin and barbiturate history, then he has heavily used barbiturates in combination with alcohol.
>
> As a child, he saw his mother beaten by the man in the house and was himself frequently and badly abused. He was a troublemaker in school, had learning difficulties, has a background of nervous disorders ranging from uncontrollably jerky fingers and very bad coordination to severe seizures. . . . He got into violent crime during his teens . . . and had a long record of youth violence by the time he became an adult.[23]

MORE SAVAGE AND WITHOUT REMORSE

Today's teenage delinquent, some experts say, is a new breed: more savage than in years past and without remorse. Journalist Jeff Coplon writes "[L]aw enforcement officials cite a chilling trend of younger criminals growing up more brutal than ever before. Propelled by poverty, anger and boredom, some of today's violent youths seem willing, even eager, to slash, stomp or shoot at the slightest show of resistance."[24]

Researchers agree. "The 'meanness quotient' is going up," said Troy Duster, as director of the Institute for the Study of Social Change at the University of California,

Berkeley. "These kids are more vicious, nastier, and more pernicious [evil]."[25]

One expert, Andrew Vachs—a lawyer, director of a juvenile maximum-security facility, and a professor—describes these kids as not caring for others. These remorseless kids learned their ways, he says, by seeing it all around them their entire lives.

> *This is the type of kid who will kill three people on separate occasions for no apparent reason . . . blowing somebody away because they looked at him wrong. . . . He simply does not feel anyone's pain but his own . . . he has no perception of the future. . . . In his world, everyone commits crimes. Everybody.*
>
> *He sees no connection between his acts and the consequences. . . . Violence permeates his existence until it is his existence. . . . Crime is . . . a way of life. . . .*
>
> *Who are his role models? Those who are, in his mind, successful criminals. . . . Pimps, dope dealers, armed robbers. . . our own "wolf children." . . . They scare the hell out of us.*[26]

YOUNGER AND YOUNGER OFFENDERS

While teen thugs are getting more violent, they are also getting younger. "Four or five years ago, even two or three years ago, it was very unusual to see a child younger than twelve or thirteen in the system particularly with multiple charges," Daniel P. Dawson, chief of a state juvenile division in Florida, told the *New York Times* in 1987 "Now you see kids aged seven, eight or nine come in with a whole string of burglaries."[27]

Younger youths are also causing more violence. Experts report an "epidemic"[28] of youth violence, especially in the past five years; says an Indianapolis prosecuting attorney in talking to Newsweek in 1993: "We're talking about younger and younger kids committing more and more serious crimes. Violence is becoming a way of life."

In 1982, for example, only 390 youths from ages 13 to 15 were arrested for murder; by 1992, that number jumped to 740.[29]

"There are some very young, very scary kids out there," says Ronald Lauder, author of Fighting Violent Crime in America. "A three-year-old was caught as she held a knife at her mother's throat. A six-year-old, blade in hand, threatened to cut off his brother's head. A seven-year-old boy got his pocket money by sudden ferocious muggings of very old women."[30]

"A ten-year-old is now like a thirteen-year-old used to be," said New Jersey police sergeant Richard J. Paraboschi. "And the sixteen-year-olds are going on forty."[31]

Most preteen violent offenders come from homes with little money. They do poorly in school, and by the time they're twelve they are years behind their classmates.[32] By twelve, more than half have emotional problems and many also suffer from nerve or psychomotor problems.[33]

"These are the children who grow up to be the violent adult predators: that 3 or 4 percent of criminals who commit 50 percent or more of the violent crimes in America,"[34] observes Ronald Lauder.

YOUTHS IN JAIL

Although the vast majority of offenders do not go to jail, more teens are in jail than ever before: more than 83,000 are in long-term juvenile correctional facilities and an estimated 2 million are in adult jails and prisons.[35]

Of the thousands of teens locked up in long-term state facilities:

- The average age is sixteen
- 93 percent are boys
- 54 percent are white, and 40 percent black
- More than 70 percent come from homes with only one parent
- Half have family members who have been locked up; 20 percent have two or more close relatives who have served time; almost one-quarter had fathers in jail or prison just in the past year
- Only 42 percent completed eighth grade, compared with 76 percent of other youths
- Almost half (48 percent) had been taking drugs or drinking when they committed the crime for which they were arrested; almost 20 percent admit to taking drugs for the first time before age ten; two out of five used drugs regularly
- About 40 percent were locked up for violent crimes such as murder and rape; 40 percent of this group had used a deadly weapon[36]

KIDS ARE VICTIMS, TOO

As kids do more of the killing, more kids are getting killed. Because guns are easy to come by, shootings are occurring at record rates. Conflicts that used to be resolved with a shrug or a punch now get settled with a handgun.

"We are losing our youth increasingly to injury and violence,"[37] said Louis Sullivan as U.S. Health and Human Services Secretary. In the past two decades, more and more of America's young have been victims of violent crimes and dying violent deaths.

Consider these chilling statistics:

- Although youth under age 20 account for about 14 percent of the American population, they comprise 30 percent of the victims of violent crimes.[38]
- Each year, almost one million teens between age 12 and 19 are raped, robbed or assaulted, often by other teens.[39] This means that about 67 out of every 1,000 teens are victims of violent crime, compared with only 26 per 1,000 persons age 20 or older.[40]
- In 1991, more than six teens were killed every day; the annual toll was more than 2,200 teenagers (under age 18) shot and killed,[41] twice as many as just five years earlier.[42]
- Three out of every ten juveniles arrested for murder in 1991 involved a victim under age 18.[43]
- Teens and children under age 18 are 244 percent more likely to be shot and killed in 1993 than they were in 1986.[44]
- In fact, an American child between age 5 and 14 is killed by a gunshot every two hours. All told, between 1979 and 1991, nearly 50,000 children were killed by guns, almost the same number as Americans killed during the entire Vietnam War.[45]
- Young black males are at greatest risk: homicide is the leading cause of death among black teens (and the second or third leading cause among young white males, depending on the year) and African-Americans are the victims of 50 percent of the homicides in this country although they represent only 12 percent of the population.[46] In other words, black youths are six times more likely to be killed than white youths.[47]
- In 1960, suicides and homicides accounted for 8 percent of youth deaths; twenty years later, they accounted for 20 percent.[48] From 1979 to 1989, the rate of suicide among teens between ages 15 to 19 increased by 35 percent. The majority, 71 percent, were committed by white males.[49]

Violence against others begins at an early age.
With the proliferation of, and easy access to,
guns, fights like this can quickly escalate
into more deadly confrontations.

Who is attacking our children? "Statistically, the killers of school-aged children are *not* for the most part sick strangers or abusive parents or criminals in the process of committing a felony, or bullies of another race," said James Mercy as chief of the Intentional Injury Section of the federal Centers for Disease Control (CDC) in Atlanta. "The killers of school-aged children are mostly other young people like themselves."[50]

Black males aged fifteen to nineteen are the most common victims of youth violence. In 1987, they were killed ten times more often than young white males, and almost always by other blacks. Black males are more than eight times more likely to be victims of violence than young white males. And contrary to popular view, most teen violence is launched against one's own race. Eighty-three percent of black teen victims were attacked by blacks; 76 percent of white teen victims were attacked by whites.[51] Violent crime among older persons was also more likely to be committed against the same race.

Interestingly, being a victim of crime is a predictor for committing crime, according to criminologist Marvin Wolfgang's long-term study of 975 boys born in Philadelphia in 1945. Violent teen criminals "often found themselves on the other side of the gun, in the role of victim. Their world appears to be characterized by almost random involvement in criminality, moving from one type of offense to another, without plan or design, being predator one day, prey the next."[52]

Why are young people so violent?

4

THE PSYCHOLOGY OF VIOLENCE AND ADOLESCENCE

These kids are . . . neglected by their parents almost from birth. They live in the street, and don't care if they live or die. They think they're worthless . . . and so they think nobody else is worth anything, either. They're filled with rage, and they take it out on anybody who looks at them sideways.[1]
—*A former probation officer from Brooklyn, N.Y.*

Before we can look at what causes violence among teenagers and children, we have to understand what causes violence in general. Although rates of violent crime in America are higher than in any other industrialized country, violence is not unique to this country or era. Ever since the beginning of recorded history, humans—but especially men—have pitted their violent nature against other humans for many reasons.

There is no one cause for violence. Violence is the result of a complex web of psychological, physiological, familial, cultural, and societal factors. Teens are even more at risk, however, because of the unique nature of adolescence.

THE PSYCHOLOGY OF VIOLENCE

Violence is the "eruption of pent-up passion," says psychotherapist and author Rollo May. But violence is but a symptom, he writes. "The disease is . . . powerlessness, insignificance, injustice."[2] Violence, he says, is merely an expression of those feelings, a way to communicate despair when words don't work or are too hard to express.

The roots of violence may be found in many emotions including:

- *Frustration.* When people can't get what they want, they feel frustrated. As frustration builds, the urge to express it aggressively grows ever stronger. Babies will scream and kick if their mother takes away a desired toy. A child may push or punch someone who prevents her from getting more candy. A teen may curse or shove another for cutting in line or flirting with a date. Violence is an extreme form of such aggressive behavior.

  But not all frustrating situations cause aggression. Nor are all people who act aggressively or violently necessarily frustrated. Other factors are involved, too.

- *Anger* is a temporary feeling that often goes hand-in-hand with frustration and sometimes causes aggression and violence. When anger gets so intense that it is overpowering, violence can erupt.

- *Hatred,* unlike anger, is a longer-lasting feeling that is often directed at a whole group or class of people, such as blacks, Jews, or foreigners. "At root it is a very violent feeling because it is a wish to injure or destroy,"[3] says psychiatrist John Gunn, who specializes in the psychology of criminal behavior.

- *Paranoia,* the unjustified feeling that someone is out to get you, also makes people violent as they try to defend themselves against an assumed threat.
- *Racism and prejudice.* Racism is the belief that a particular race is better than another. Prejudice is when someone has hostile feelings or attitudes toward others because they belong to certain racial, religious, or national groups, or because of their sex, age, education, or any other factor—even their eating habits or dressing style. Prejudice works by assuming that because people are different, they are worse.

  Bigots, people who are intolerant of those who are different, are typically suspicious and paranoid. They feel threatened by people of other races, threatened that *they* will get all the good jobs and nice homes. Such "ethnocentrism"—the belief that one's own ethnic roots are the best or the only "right" or "normal" ones—feeds both fear and paranoia, which can generate hate and, in turn, trigger violence.

  When a person or a group feels frustrated that they are not getting what they feel they deserve, they may feel the need to blame someone. Historically, people have blamed other ethnic groups for their bad luck. These innocent victims are called scapegoats. As a group's frustration grows, it may take out its frustration-aggression on scapegoats.
- *Powerlessness.* When individuals feel they cannot improve their lives, their self-esteem plummets, that is, they feel they have little self-worth. They feel insignificant, unimportant, and powerless.

"No human being can exist for long without some sense of his own significance," writes May. "Deeds of violence in our society are performed largely by those trying to establish their self-esteem, to defend their self-image, and to demonstrate that they, too, are significant."[4]

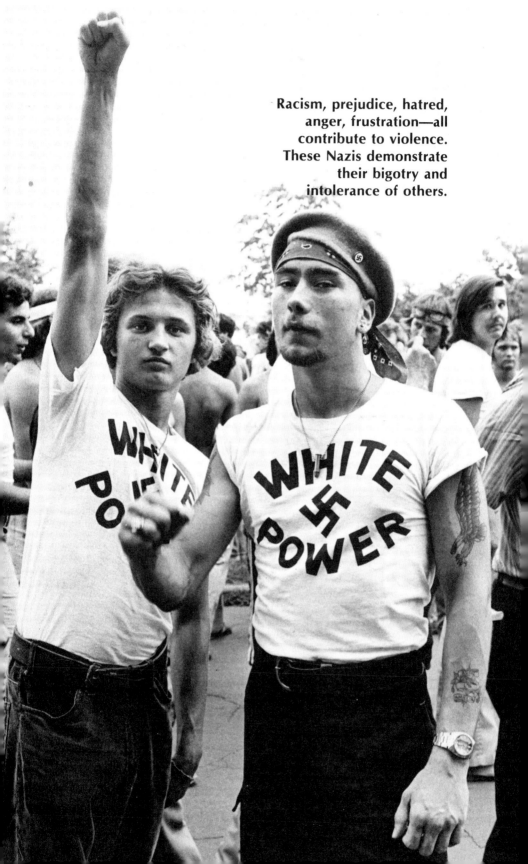

Racism, prejudice, hatred, anger, frustration—all contribute to violence. These Nazis demonstrate their bigotry and intolerance of others.

Violence in America, he says, is largely a cry for self-recognition, a statement to prove that one is significant and has the power to make an impact.

When an entire race is victimized by racism and prejudice and forced to live in poverty with dim prospects for a better future, the victims are bound to feel frustrated, powerless, and worthless. This is a breeding ground for violence, May says, as feelings of impotence (of having no power) build up and the need to seize some kind of power grows.

> When a person (or a group of people) has been denied over a period of time what he feels are his legitimate rights, when he is continuously burdened with feelings of impotence which corrode any remaining self-esteem, violence is the predictable end result. Violence is an explosion of the drive to destroy that which is interpreted as the barrier to one's self-esteem, movement, and growth. This desire to destroy may so completely take over the person that any object that gets in the way is destroyed.[5]

As frustration builds, causing anger and hatred, aggressive urges may push a person out of control.

> One's mind becomes foggy, and perception of the enemy becomes unclear; one loses awareness of the environment and wants only to act out this inner compulsion to do violence, come what may. . . . [Violence is a way to] prove one's power, to establish the worth of the self. . . . No desire or time to think is left once the violence breaks out. . . .[6]

May points out that when powerless persons suddenly realize they do have some power, such as the power to do harm to others, the feeling can be thrilling though the results tragic.

THE BIOLOGY OF VIOLENCE

Some experts believe that aggression is a biologically programmed impulse in men, particularly young men, either as part of their genetic makeup or caused by male hormones.

In either case, most youths learn how to control these aggressive impulse through sports, physical labor and verbal arguing. Those who don't, however, act aggressively. When young boys, four to ten years old, hit others, show anger frequently, defy parents and teachers, act destructively by throwing things, and/or steal or commit other petty crimes for more than six months, they are considered too aggressive. Researchers have found that these children are three times more likely to become criminals at a later age.[7]

Violent tendencies may also find their roots in biological abnormalities. Researchers have found that violent criminals have a higher percentage of neurological (nervous system) problems than others. These include seizures and brain damage—even minor brain damage, head injury, and abnormal brain waves.[8] In fact, some of the most violent children have severely abnormal brain waves.[9] Often, brain damage and head injury are the results of child abuse; even shaking a child can cause brain hemorrhages that may develop into behavior problems and later into violence.

A 1989 study that tracked ninety-five jailed juvenile delinquents for seven years found, for example, that those who grew up to be the most violent not only had a family history of abuse but also suffered from serious neurological damage. Whereas family violence may set the stage for a child to be violent, physical problems may impair his ability to control his violent impulses.[10]

Recently researchers claimed to have found strong evidence that some people may be born with a greater tendency toward violence. As researchers uncover genetic clues to a wide array of mental disorders, they have begun to suspect that a tendency toward violence may be one of them. Although no one single gene can be responsible for violence, many scientists believe that a person's genetic makeup could make them more prone to commit violence. If a father is impulsive and aggressive, for example, researchers from the Medical College of Pennsylvania estimate that there is a 25 to 40 percent chance that his son or daughter will inherit that tendency toward violence.

The subject has provoked much controversy. Some projects have been criticized for seeking genetic causes of violence, rather than examining the economic and social causes of violence. The National Institutes of Mental Health, a government agency, had announced such a program called the "violence initiative," but protests from critics successfully stopped the project. Dr. Peter Bregin has compared the violence initiative to genetic research programs in Nazi Germany.

Other recent research suggests that the human brain has the ability to adapt to its environment. If a young child lives in an area where gunfire constantly rattles the windows and violence occurs on an everyday basis, or if a child is a victim of abuse or neglect by his or her family, the brain may physically adapt to that environment. When the world is frightening, as in a state of war, the brain pumps out stress chemicals to help prepare the person for battle and survival. When children experience this fright, their brain reacts in a similar way, producing chemicals that make a person more aggressive. Several studies, for example, have shown that men who commit impulsive violence, such as murdering a stranger, have different levels of brain chemicals than other men. Researchers are investigating whether these changes may become permanent changes that are passed on to the next generation, making it more likely to be aggressive and violent.

"[W]e are all beginning to conclude that the bad environments that more and more children are being exposed to are, indeed, creating an epidemic of violence. Environmental events are really causing molecular changes in the brain so that people are more impulsive," says Dr. Markus J. Kruesi of the Institute for Juvenile Research at the University of Illinois in Chicago.[11]

Experts point out that these changes in the brain may be contributing to the greater levels of violence committed by girls in recent years. "Some researchers believe that the increase in female criminal violence since the 1960s could be an early sign of how the genes of violence already are building up in the population," reports the *Chicago Tribune* in 1993.[12] Experts note that each generation since the 1950s has been more violent. One theory holds that as aggressive men have children, they pass on their aggressive tendency. As their children grow up in stress-torn families and neighborhoods, they become even more prone to violence. If they then mate with a person whose father was also aggressive, the next child will be even more aggressive and prone to violence.

Some experts predict that within 25 years, biological and genetic tests may be able to identify children with a violent tendency. All of this is not to say that people are born to be violent and there's nothing we can do about it. In fact, the evidence points out that it is the environments in which children grow up that trigger their violent tendencies. "A child with a fearless personality may turn into a criminal if reared in a chaotic home, but given a stable upbringing, he could well become a CEO [chief executive officer of a company], test pilot, entrepreneur [business person], or the next Bill Clinton," claims Jerome Kagan, a Harvard psychologist.[13]

ADOLESCENCE AND HOW IT RELATES
TO VIOLENCE

As children approach their teens, their lives turn upside down. Hormones rage, wreaking havoc on moods and temperament. As their bodies change, young teens spend ever more time obsessed, insecure, and anxious about their self-image and attractiveness.

At the same time, they grapple with who they really are and what they think, breaking away from their parents and being more independent, becoming more competent, and learning about intimacy with the other sex.

Entering junior high marks an adolescent's entrance to teen culture. Many feel an urgency to act differently, try new values, compare themselves to different people—urges that may get them into trouble.

Peers become ever more important: "Much of the power of peer pressure at this age derives from an almost desperate eagerness for acceptance and a sense of belonging," [14] says Harvard psychiatrist Beatrix Hamburg. Eager to experiment, young teens grow vulnerable to good as well as bad influences.

As youngsters navigate their way through the turbulent waters of adolescence, undergoing profound physical, intellectual, and emotional changes, their self-image and self-esteem are fragile and in a constant state of change. They may be unpredictable, inconsistent, hotheaded, rebellious, and, at times, scared but trying hard not to show it.

"A normal adolescent isn't a normal adolescent if he acts normal," says psychoanalyst and author Judith Viorst. Adolescence, she says, is "when our body and our psyche start coming unglued, when our normal teenage state is sometimes hard to distinguish from a state of insanity, when development—normal development—demands that we lose and leave and let go of . . . everything." [15]

Adolescence "is an agonizing time for most people," says Felton Earls, professor of psychology at Washington University School of Medicine, even for those from supportive families and schools.[16] But, says sociologist David Bakan, most struggle through it, believing in "the promise" up ahead, "that if a young person does all the things he is 'supposed to do' during his adolescence, he will then realize success, status, income, power . . . in his adulthood."[17]

But for those who do not have the luxury of a loving, nurturing family, an attentive school, and a supportive community, life is different. For them, "the adolescent's confrontation with the demands of adapting to a highly competitive, complex, racist environment is awesome,"[18] says Earls.

Although many teens, perhaps the majority, have the urge to act violently, most learn nonviolent coping skills to express their anger and frustration. These include verbal responses, compromises, taking constructive action to improve their situation, or expressing their anger through sports, music, or art.

But some teenagers don't learn these skills, either because their parents didn't teach them or because they are impaired and unable to express themselves verbally. Instead, they resort to physical expressions of their anger. And some just give up, realizing that they are not going to be able to reap the "rewards" in society.

Others, giving up on their future, find that the only way to save face and make up for their sagging self-esteem and feelings of worthlessness is to demand respect from others.

"The respect the kids demand is compensation for the very little courtesy they really receive in their lives," Joyce Ladner, professor of social work at Howard University, told the *Washington Post*. Many kids on the street may act brave but actually suffer from very low self-esteem. "Almost anything can ruffle them"[19]

Some children and teenagers living in inner cities must prove to others that they are tough and ruthless to prevent being picked on by others.

When deprived teenagers don't know how to cope constructively with frustration and the aggressive tendencies swell up inside, they may "resort to macho displays of violence to preserve a 'twisted sense of dignity,' "[20] said John A. Calhoun, then executive director of the National Crime Prevention Council. In other words some kids are violent to save face and to release their pent-up frustration and rage.

Teenagers kill over such petty things as jackets, radios, seats in the movies, and even just passing comments. One chilling trend is the killing of other teens in attempts to rob them of fashionable clothes, including athletic and bomber jackets and shoes, such as Air Jordans—a line of Nikes endorsed by the popular Chicago Bulls star.

Typically, teenagers "test" and taunt one another to see who can get the upper hand or to find out what another's limits are. They'll fight over honor, possessions, or territory. With guns so available and drugs putting so much at stake, what used to be a fistfight is now a shoot-out.

As shootings become more and more common, they seem almost "normal" to teens who witness them. As a result, the thought of shooting someone comes to be thought of as a "normal" reaction to feelings of anger, revenge or frustration.

In their own turbulent search for self-identity, many violent adolescents show "little if any concern for the physical injury or harm inflicted . . . little empathy for the victims,"[21] say Syracuse University sociologists Cheryl Carpenter and Barry Glassner. In fact, they tend "to . . . deny the actual harm to victims that they impose." When victims fight back, the teen assailants may get more violent and justify it by believing that the victims deserved the violence or brought it on themselves.

Pete, a juvenile offender in reform school who is guilty of five armed robberies and three aggravated assaults, explains casually, "If we got to shoot you, we shoot you. It's done in anger. You're playing hero, and we get upset. It burns us up. We're serious, and you think this is a joke. You're testing us." [22]

Some teens glamorize the violence, and believe, sometimes accurately, that their peers will think better of them if they commit a brutal crime and are caught. One 17-year-old, arrested with five friends for raping and strangling two young girls in Houston, supposedly said to a friend upon arrest: "Hey, great! We've hit the big time." [23]

But some teenagers get into trouble merely because they are bored and seeking the thrill of getting away with something. "Delinquency provides a kick that is missing from the easy consumerism of daily life," [24] says sociologist Clemens Bartollas. In proving their "manliness" to each other, some teens may find themselves committing violent acts just to prove to each other how "cool" they can be.

Yet no matter how stressful, deprived, or boring adolescence is for some young people, *most* teenagers do not respond violently. Quite often, the violent teenager has *learned* that violence is the way to cope with anger and frustration. The most powerful place to learn violence is in the family. And when violence is glorified by the culture, as it is in America, it becomes easier to understand why our country is besieged by a wave of teen violence.

5

THE LEGACY OF FAMILY VIOLENCE

Home is where the hurt is.[1]
—Time *magazine*

We've seen how poverty and prejudice can cause frustration, anger, and powerlessness, and how these emotions can cause violence. We've also seen why teenagers, coping with the stormy changes of adolescence, may be particularly more violence-prone than others.

But people don't live in isolation. They live in families which, in all too many cases, are violent. These families live in communities which are either strong and supportive or disruptive and chaotic. These communities are part of a larger culture that seems to depict and glorify violence in its media every day, everywhere.

FAMILY VIOLENCE

When parents are violent with each other or with their children, research shows that the children grow up at much greater risk of being violent, too. According to Dr. Larry Hebert, an expert on child abuse and violence, "Although the family traditionally has been viewed as an institution that serves to diminish violence in our society, the truth is that the family serves as a breeding ground for the life cycle of violence in about 50 percent of our American homes."[2]

For many families, "home, sweet home" is but a myth. *Every day,* throughout the United States, in families rich and poor, violence—child abuse, child sexual abuse, and spouse abuse—occurs about 17,000 times.[3] In fact, "violence seems as typical of family relationships as love. . . . Starting with slaps and going on to torture and murder, the family provides a prime setting for every degree of physical violence,"[4] say family violence experts Suzanne Steinmetz and Murray Straus.

When children are abused, they never know when they are going to be cuddled or kicked, hugged or hit. Such children grow up feeling rejected, angry, and with poor self-esteem and low self-image. As adolescents, they may take out their anger and pain on their parents or other victims. As adults, they are much more likely to commit violence.

Further, when parents "solve" their problems through violence, it's a sign that they are out of control, unable to teach their kids how to cope constructively with anger and frustration. Then, the children learn to use violence to settle arguments or to control others.

Children who are harshly punished on a regular basis are also more likely to become violent, according to a 1993 American Psychological Association report called, Violence and Youth." Such punishment, the report says, breeds a cycle of violence. Although the child may cooperate more in the short-term, harsh punishment is more likely to make the child aggressive in the long run. The report cites a 22-year study of 875 children starting at age 8. Children who were harshly punished were more aggressive with their playmates, shoving and starting fistfights. As adults, they were much more likely to be violent, have criminal records, and become parents who, in turn, harshly punish their own children.[5]

Abuse can be even more powerful in turning a child toward violence. Children who are beaten and abused may develop aggressive and angry thought patterns that interfere with their ability to act calmly in a conflict. As early as age 8, such boys will act stubbornly and defiantly; by 12, they start bullying others. By 14, they may lie, cheat, steal, and fight with others. Soon, their pent-up anger at childhood abuse expresses itself in full-blown violent behavior.

This scenario shows how children with violent parents become violent parents themselves, as the cycle of violence gets passed from one generation to the next.

FAMILY VIOLENCE AND TEEN CRIME

Whether children are abused themselves or stand by as innocent witnesses watching one parent abuse another, the effect seems to be equally powerful in boosting the odds that the children will imitate the violent behavior they grew up with.

Many studies of juvenile delinquents show a family history of abuse; likewise, may studies of adult criminals, many of whom started their criminal careers as juveniles, indicate family histories of abuse. For example:

- A 1978 study of 3,636 New York State delinquents showed that they had been abused five times more than nondelinquents.[6]
- A Yale University study showed that about 30 percent of children who had been beaten grew up to be violent adults, either beating their own children or their parents, compared with only 3 percent of other adults who had not been beaten as children.[7]
- A 1989 study looked at ninety-five jailed juvenile

delinquents, most very violent. Eighty had been victims of severe family violence or had seen such violence throughout their childhood.[8]
- A study of 237 prison inmates found that 87 percent of those reporting severely abusive parents were violent criminals.[9]
- Another study found that 85 percent of teen murderers had been severely beaten as children.[10]

"Many criminologists are convinced that the cruel violent adult has learned his unpleasant characteristics from his parents," concludes forensic psychiatrist John Gunn. In other words, he says, "if people are surrounded by violence and brutality, you can expect them to behave in a similar way."[11]

Dr. Jerome Miller, former director of a youth corrections department, has interviewed hundreds of youngsters involved in horrible random crimes of violence. He claims that every single one came from an abnormal family. "These kids don't fall out of the sky, and they don't fall out of normal families. They have been subjected almost always to a huge amount of sexual abuse, of physical abuse. They witness violence coming and going."[12]

FAMILY VIOLENCE AND FEMALE TEEN CRIME

Although girls and women have always been less aggressive than males, an overwhelming percentage of female criminals also had previously been victims of abuse. For example:

- A 1982 study of 192 female delinquents found that 79 percent had been victims of physical abuse, 32 percent had been sexually abused by parents or close relatives, and 50 percent had been victims of rape.[13]
- A 1983 study of adult women in prison found that almost all had been victims of physical and/or sex-

ual abuse as children; more than 60 percent had been sexually abused, and half had been raped.[14]

Many young women who are abused run away from home and get involved in prostitution and street crime.

FRACTURED FAMILIES, FRACTURED VALUES

Although poverty is often blamed for violence, researchers stress that the family is a much more powerful factor. When two teenagers viciously attacked five children in their neighborhood, for example, leaving them for dead, Harvard psychologists commented that such adolescent random violence is mostly caused by "shallow emotional attachments first to their parents and then to society in general. . . . Very few people are driven to violent crime by poverty. The crucial test . . . is how they are raised and the presence or absence of character and conscience."[15]

Throughout history, many ethnic and immigrant groups have worked their way out of poverty. "If the number of black adolescent boys growing up on the streets and turning to crime is growing, it is not because they are poor but because they are fatherless and without families,"[16] says Rita Kramer, author of *At a Tender Age*.

Kramer points out that the epidemic of teenage mothers giving birth to another generation of unprepared teenage mothers is breeding a generation of psychologically damaged boys, many prone to crime, and girls destined to become yet another generation of teen mothers.

Broken families, teenage mothers, and absent fathers can profoundly influence a teen's direction away from or toward violence. Male teens need good male role models to show them how to be "a man" without being violent. Yet more than two-thirds of all black children are born to unmarried women half of whom are teenagers. In the heart of New York's inner city, 80 percent of the babies are born to unwed women. Nationally, almost one-third of births are out of wedlock.

In addition to such high rates of single women giving birth, the United States has the highest divorce rate in the world. All told, three-quarters of poor black children have absent fathers;[17] two-thirds of all young black children and one-quarter of all American children live in single-parent households where the parent is almost always the mother. And 70 percent of teens in criminal detention come from either single-parent or no-parent homes.[18]

"The basic problem is clearly . . . children having children, without any thought about having them or any ability to nurture them,"[19] said Richard Garmise, as psychologist for Family Court in New York City.

Once youngsters reach thirteen or fourteen, many don't want their mothers telling them what to do. Without a man around to provide a strong role model, young fatherless teens take to the streets, where drug dealers, dope runners, or gang members become their role models.

"In your ghetto neighborhoods, the guy who's the toughest is your neighborhood hero," says Ray Simmons, an ex-convict who now runs Operation Prison Gap, a bus service in New York for families of prisoners. He is trying to start a counseling service for ghetto youngsters. "The badder you are, the more acceptable you are. And it's because their value system is backwards."[20]

THE DECLINE OF ADOLESCENT WELL-BEING

Some sociologists believe that the well-being of all adolescents is declining. More teens live in divorced families, in which they find themselves either without fathers or being shuffled between parents and coping with stepparents. Many youngsters feel resentful and rejected in such circumstances.

The rise of teenage mothers is spawning yet another generation of children from broken, dysfunctional homes— this, in turn, can lead to increased teenage crime.

More discussions between fathers and sons might help slow down the epidemic of violent crime perpetrated by teenage boys.

Even among intact families, many fathers spend little time with their children. At the same time, mothers have streamed into the labor force in record numbers:

> As men and women increase their commitment to their own self-fulfillment, they . . . reduce their commitment to sacrificing personal pursuits for their children's welfare. . . . Parents are becoming available at times convenient to the parents, not at times when the child has the most need for attention.[21]

Middle-class and upper-class kids who seem to have everything may come to think that they are entitled to anything, are above the law, and can do as they please, even if it means hurting other people. As more parents lead harried life-styles, they supervise their teenagers less and offer less guidance in instilling values.

"Neglect is abuse," Randa Dembroff, then an official with the Los Angeles County Bar Association, told *Time*. "A workaholic parent is just as abusive as one who physically abuses his children."[22]

Neglect, in fact, is far more common than abuse, and can also be devastating to a child. "We have a whole generation of kids suffering from neglect," said Rice University sociologist Stephen Klineberg in *Time* magazine. "There is no one at home when they return from school, and this neglect in socialization results in increased violence."[23]

Furthermore, while the educational performance of teens has slipped, delinquency, pregnancy, and drug and alcohol use have soared. Some researchers conclude that as the bond between parent and child weakens, as they believe it has since 1960, "the proportion of adolescents behaving in ways destructive to themselves and to others grows ever larger."[24]

As divorces, single-parent homes, and two-parent career families keep increasing, children learn more of their values outside the home. Ruth Begun, a founder of the Society for Prevention of Violence and a researcher on violence, points out that many parents don't know how and/or don't have the time to teach values to their children.

"Bored, some kids turn to television, others to the streets, where the role models are often other kids—and where might often makes right," [25] reports journalist Stephen Sawicki.

Time reports:

> *As a consequence of indifference and abuse, children are left emotional cripples, self-centered, angry and alienated. And fated to repeat the chilling lessons they have learned. "These children are dead inside," says [forensic] psychologist [Shawn] Johnston. "For them to feel alive and important, they engage in terrible types of sadistic activity."* [26]

The breakdown of the family, the community and the culture can be powerful influences in putting teens at risk for violent behavior.

6

THE IMPACT OF COMMUNITY AND CULTURE ON TEEN VIOLENCE

Today's children, unlike those of earlier generations, are fed a steady diet of glorified violence. . . . By the age of sixteen, the typical child has witnessed an estimated 200,000 acts of violence, including 33,000 murders. Inevitably, contend many experts, some youngsters will imitate the brutality in real life.[1]

—Time *magazine*

INFLUENCE OF THE COMMUNITY

When families break down, the community has historically stepped in to fill the gap, providing children and teenagers with positive role models and experiences. Yet, community institutions—extended families, religious and civic organizations, and good schools—have weakened in recent years. "Many studies reveal that increases in crime and violence are signals that the front-line institutions—family, school, church and civic groups—have failed to hold,"[2] said John A. Calhoun of the National Crime Prevention Council.

Neighborhoods and communities in the inner city especially are failing to provide positive environments for teenagers. In the past, communities were strong and cohesive, even in ghettos. Children not only felt that they were part of their community or neighborhood, but also part of a culture. The child's ethnic background and family's traditions gave the child a sense of identity, patterns of behavior to follow, and a feeling of being part of a larger group. Among minorities, strong cultural and religious values can protect a child against the potentially damaging effects of a harsh life and environment. But today, closely knit neighborhoods have been unraveled by soaring rates of crime, substance abuse, teenage pregnancy, and single-parent families. Rising unemployment, inflation, reduced services for the poor, AIDS, dwindling police resources, deteriorating schools, homelessness, crack, and widespread gun accessibility have all fractured the community.

Instead of turning to community leaders and positive role models in the community, youths turn ever more to gangs for protection, a sense of identity, and a place to belong.

For many children, such as those in inner-city housing projects, their community is riddled by daily gunfire. For the country's 5.3 million children living in poverty in inner-city neighborhoods, daily life means daily violence. A special assistant to the former U.S. surgeon general said, "These children are surrounded by a very real and immediate world of violence, of gunfire, of death. It's every day. We just simply didn't have that before." [3]

Almost 17 percent of youngsters ages 10 to 17, say they have seen or known someone who has been shot. [4] In one Chicago housing project every three days a person is beaten, shot, or stabbed. [5] Children in such projects have nightmares, personality disorders, and bouts of depression. While some give up and withdraw, others become aggressive themselves.

Childhood poverty itself is considered the most important factor for putting young Americans at risk for long-term problems, including drugs and crime. One in five American children lives in poverty—15 percent of white children and a staggering 45 percent and 39 percent for black and Hispanic children, respectively.[6] To a great extent, said the federal report of the 1990 National Commission on Children, childhood poverty sets children up for reaching adulthood unhealthy, illiterate, and unemployable.

Historically, neighborhoods and communities have been able to uphold traditional values and morals in spite of poverty. Yet some experts point to the decline of positive values in American society. "Fifty years ago there was a clear American moral and civic identity," wrote columnist William Pfaff in the *Los Angeles Times*. But the Vietnam War, affluence, television, the decline of the churches, pop culture, and growing crime rates have left "America a morally isolated people, no longer connected to a culture deeper or more responsible than that provided by the mass entertainment industry." Pfaff blames teenage violence committed "for fun" on this moral void.[7]

Laments Barbara Tuchman, author and historian, "We have lost a sense of respect for serious, honest conduct . . . somehow people don't take wrongdoing seriously. . . . We're not surprised anymore. We're just used to it."[8]

Some people say we just don't know right from wrong anymore. Instead of having righteous, moral heroes, our idols have become athletes, movie stars, and business tycoons, some of whom we later find out are swindlers and liars. The demise of American idealism, some people say, provides the context in which teenagers, bored and/or angry, may lash out in violence.

Compounding the problems created by the breakdowns in community and traditional values is the new

The deteriorating environment many children live
in does little to improve self-esteem, self-respect,
or hope. Poverty like this breeds violent crime.

set of values among youths for whom prison is a badge of honor and respect among peers. As *Newsweek* (August 2, 1993) reported, "Prison is the dominant institution shaping the culture, replacing church and school." With more young black men going to prison than to college, and often following in the footsteps of their fathers and uncles, many come to think of juvenile prison as "a kind of sleep-away camp" where friends are living, the look is "hip," and doing time is a ticket to respect when you get back on the street.[9]

THE INFLUENCE OF VIOLENCE IN OUR CULTURE

Violence assaults our senses every day through the mass media. American youngsters not only watch about four hours of action-packed TV every day but they see ads for and play with G.I. Joe dolls and machine guns, Teenage Mutant Ninja Turtles, and violent electronic video games of Nintendo, Sega, and others. In fact, war toys are a billion-dollar industry in this country.

As kids become adolescents, the exposure to violence doesn't abate. On television, in music, and in movies, teenagers in particular witness violence almost every day.

"Most of us see so much violence on television that we almost do not notice it any longer,"[10] says author Gilda Berger in *Violence and the Media*. Yet, one hour of prime-time television, such as the program "Hunter," NBC's big 1988 hit, had twenty-three violent acts per episode. "Wiseguy" on CBS had forty-three violent acts.[11]

Nearly nine out of ten hours of family prime-time TV episodes have violence. Even Saturday-morning cartoons, geared to young children, are chock-full of violence—about twenty-five violent acts each hour.[12] Even the news has gotten more violent—in 1993, network television coverage of violence had *doubled,* according to a study by the Center for Media and Public Affairs.[13]

Many studies have looked at whether TV violence is linked to aggression. Although findings have been controversial, they lean heavily toward a causal relationship between viewing violent acts on TV and committing violence in real life. "The consensus among most of the research community is that violence on television does lead to aggressive behavior by children and teenagers who watch the programs," concluded the 1983 National Institute of Mental Health report, which reviewed 2,500 research projects on TV violence.[14] A 1993 report by the American Psychological Association agreed when it stated that "viewing violence increases violence."[15]

Studies show that violence on television not only incites real-life violence, but makes us less sensitive to violence and its effects; it also tends to glamorize violence as well as make viewers think of violence as normal. Frequent TV viewers also tend to see the world as meaner and more hostile and dangerous than occasional TV viewers. Thinking that the world is mean, people who watch a lot of TV are more apt to react violently when provoked, researchers have observed.

Popular movies are laden with violence, too. The "splatter" and "slasher" movies—horror movies such as *Friday the 13th, Nightmare on Elm Street, I Spit on Your Grave,* and *Splatter University*—depict murder, torture, and mutilation, and fascinate many teenagers. Such films are booming in video rentals, especially rentals by eleven- to fifteen-year-olds.[16] All-night "gross out" parties feature three or four such movies in a row. Some stars from these movies have become cult heroes.

By the end of elementary school, the typical child, according to the American Psychological Association, has watched about 100,000 violent acts, including 38,000 murders.[17] Kids may be not only more apt to

Violent videos lure young customers. Many people believe that the proliferation of movies, television programs, and music videos that glamorize violence desensitizes people to the cruelty of its actual effects.

imitate such violence but also more likely to disregard the pain and suffering of real victims, for TV victims rarely bleed or suffer.

Some rock music, too, has a violent pulse. Symbolizing adolescent rebellion and teen culture, much of today's rock, heavy metal, and rap music glorify hate, abuse, sexual deviance, and violence. Heavy metal bands such as Slayer, King Diamond, Megadeth, and Venom share themes of torture, murder, rape, hatred, and substance abuse.

Heavy metal music has even been linked to several murders and suicides. Although the music obviously didn't cause the deaths, some experts believe it played a powerful role in influencing the young and impressionable killers.

The West Coast serial murderer known as the "Night Stalker," for example, is said to have been obsessed with AC/DC, a heavy metal band. A fourteen-year-old girl, also obsessed with heavy metal, stabbed her mother to death after listening to such music. A nineteen-year-old was listening to Ozzy Osbourne, whose album included "Suicide Solution," when he got up and shot himself in the head. He was still wearing his headphones.

Rap music, too, is infamous for its violent allusions. Musician Ice-T, for example, has a record cover showing a gun shoved into a man's mouth. Ice-T's trademark is a golden gun pendant hanging from a gold chain.

Music videos shown on cable TV twenty-four hours a day also depict violence slickly and smoothly. In two studies of rock videos, 55 percent had violent themes. And viewers were found to be less sensitive to violence right after watching them[18]

Many video games for teens are becoming more realistic and gruesome. *Mortal Kombat,* for example, allows players to cut the heads off opponents or to rip out their heart and other organs. In *Lethal Enforcers,* you can shoot the bad guys, and the innocent people, as well. In *Mad Dog McCree,* if you don't shoot first, you'll get gunned down by the gunslinging fellow on the screen.

Although television, music, and movies are rarely considered the only cause of violence, many experts agree that such exposure to violence, day in and day out, may be making us insensitive, perhaps immune, to human pain. These media also glorify violence, making it seem macho, sexy, exciting, erotic, and perhaps even rewarding. All these not-so-subtle messages may be helping to promote violence among our teenagers.

Although television programs do not have ratings for violence, movies and music now do, and, by the end of 1994, the video industry will rate video games voluntarily.

Even today's pop psychology has been blamed for the rise in violent crimes. Messages, such as "Be assertive" and "Don't feel guilty; guilt is bad," could lead some people to feel even less concern for others. "For those who already lack the capacity for remorse, who lack a strong moral sense of what is right or wrong, this is giving them license to commit hideous crimes,"[19] says sociologist Jack Levin of Northeastern University, the author of a book on mass murders.

In addition to all the influences from pop culture on teenagers, a 1990 report from a commission formed by the National Association of State Boards of Education and the American Medical Association stated that never before has a generation of teens been so plagued by problems, been less healthy—emotionally and physically—and less cared for. As a result, many teens are ill prepared to become successful adults, the report said.[20]

In spite of violent families and violence in the mass media, teen crimes wouldn't be as lethal if it weren't for guns. And if it weren't for drugs, many kids wouldn't be so apt to pull the trigger.

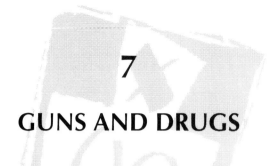

7

GUNS AND DRUGS

How can America think of itself as a civilized society when day after day the bodies pile up amid the primitive crackle of gunfire across the land?
—Time *magazine, July 17, 1989*

There's no doubt about it, we are a heavily armed society. Our population is about 260 million—we have more than 201 million guns in the country.[1] Gun ownership is so widespread in our free and liberal land that there is one gun for every other household. Many youngsters can grab a gun as easily as a peanut butter and jelly sandwich. With a gun on hand at the critical moment, temporary problems too often turn into permanent tragedies.

Consider these chilling statistics:

- Since the beginning of the century, three-quarters of a million people have been shot dead in the U.S. with privately owned guns; that's 30 percent more than have been killed in all the wars in which America has been involved.[2] One-third of those people killed by guns, or one-quarter of a million Americans, died in the 1980s; that's four times more people than were killed in the Vietnam War.[3]

- In 1990, 38,317 Americans were shot;[4] more people die of gunshot wounds every two years than have died so far from AIDS or in the entire Vietnam War.[5]
- Six of every ten killings in the U.S. involve guns.[6] One of every four deaths of teenagers is caused by a gunshot.[7]
- Every day more than 100,000 kids tote a gun to school.[8]
- Every day, 14 children aged eighteen and younger are killed by guns.[9] Since 1986, gunshot wounds to children sixteen and younger have soared more than 300 percent in urban areas.[10]
- In 1987, 3,392 children aged eighteen and younger were killed by guns;[11] In 1990, 4,200 were shot and killed;[12] in 1992, more than 5,100.[13]
- Juveniles' use of guns in homicides increased from 64 percent to 78 percent between 1987 and 1991, during which time juvenile arrests for weapons violations increased by 62 percent.[14]

Around the country, youngsters use guns. "City streets have become flooded with unregistered and untraceable handguns, available to anyone of any age with a bit of cash,"[15] reports Newsweek. In many cities, guns can even be rented on credit for the evening.

In the inner cities, some 35 percent of teens report they carry guns, at least occasionally.[16] And the gun culture is not just in the inner cities. According to a 1993 Harris poll of 2,508 students in 96 schools across the country, 15 percent of the sixth to twelfth graders said they had brought a handgun to school in the past month; 11 percent said they had been shot at and 59 percent said they could get a gun if they wanted one.[17]

For many teens these days, using a gun is *the* way to settle an argument: " 'Why would you fight somebody when you can shoot 'em?', a bespectacled sixteen-year-old asked incredulously, 'Instead of fighting, it's easier to shoot,' " the boy told the *Washington Post*. " 'If you fight, you could be there all day,' " said his friend. " 'You could just shoot 'em and get it over with.' "[18]

Handguns, automatic and semiautomatic rifles and machine guns, teflon bullets that go through bulletproof vests, and plastic guns that can't be spotted by metal detectors are just a few of the weapons that are blanketing the American landscape and finding their way into the hands of children, hotheaded teenagers, hate groups, drug dealers, and gangs. Homicides, suicides, armed robberies, and gun accidents are so common that they often don't even make the local news.

The United States of America is, in fact, the only modern industrialized nation in the world that widely and lawfully allows its citizens to freely own and even stockpile firearms. "The only such nation . . . so attached to the supposed 'right' to bear arms that its laws abet [help] assassins, professional criminals, berserk murderers, and political terrorists at the expense of the orderly population,"[19] says historian Richard Hofstadter.

In 1992, for example, handguns killed 33 people in Britain, 60 in Japan and 128 in Canada. In the United States, handguns were used to murder 13,220 people, according to the Handgun Control organization and the Center to Prevent Handgun Violence.[20]

To many teenagers, especially those living in inner cities, guns have become an acceptable part of daily life, a ticket to more money, self-esteem, status, and power. "There is a cultural pattern in the community [in Detroit] that makes the carrying of guns an accepted and normal kind of behavior,"[21] reports Marvin Zalman of the Criminal Justice Department at Wayne State University in Detroit.

Explains *Time* magazine: "With a $25 investment, all the teasing from classmates stops cold. Suddenly, the shortest, ugliest, and weakest kid becomes a player."[22]

At least 18 states already have laws that prohibit juveniles from having guns, and Congress is considering making the ban national. In 1994, the federal Brady law went into effect amid much controversy. The law now requires a five-day waiting period to buy a handgun, and during that time a background check on the person wishing to buy the gun is to be conducted. While supporters of the law believe that it will prevent persons with criminal records, drug addicts, and the mentally ill from getting handguns, opponents claim that the bill will do little to prevent violent crime and that the law is unconstitutional.

Opponents of the Brady law also claim that it won't stop criminals who really want guns and can buy them on the street, and that the legislation focuses on guns rather than on criminals. Those opposed to the law say that tougher jail sentences, more prisons, and more police on the streets would be a far more effective way to fight crime than a law that tries to control guns.

In the meantime, the Clinton administration in 1994 also declared semiautomatic shotguns to be "destructive weapons." Now owners of these firearms must register them and be fingerprinted and photographed by local police.

In addition, a new bill, Brady II, has been introduced to Congress. This bill proposes a ban on the manufacture and sale of many semiautomatic assault weapons, requires licensing and fingerprinting, and a seven-day waiting period for all gun purchases as well, allowing only one weapon to be purchased a month per person. It would also raise annual fees for gun dealers from $66 to $1,000. All these efforts are intended to limit the number and kinds of weapons on the streets of America, but such legislation is expected to make only a dent.

DRUGS AND VIOLENCE

Compounding the problem of kids having easy access to guns is the soaring use of street drugs. The *New York Times* reports: "Experts attribute the increase in killings to a complex variety of factors. . . . Most often cited is drug use and its culture, including the tendency of newer drugs to cause aggression among addicts and the potential for huge profits by organized gangs of dealers." [23]

Studies have found, for example, that people who use illegal drugs (heroin, cocaine, PCP, etc.) commit four to six times as many crimes as those who don't use drugs. Looking at it from the other side, half of those arrested for crimes are drug users. [24]

When juvenile records in state detention centers were reviewed in 1988, authorities found that half of those arrested for violent crimes were under the influence of drugs or alcohol when they committed their crime. [25]

Many kids start trying drugs as early as the fourth grade. As soon as they buy illegal drugs, they become part of a drug culture that is linked to violence at every turn, from addicts preying on the innocent for money to buy drugs to savage wars among drug kingpins.

"Territorial disputes between rival drug dealers, robberies, violent retaliations, elimination of informers, punishment for selling adulterated, phony or otherwise 'bad' drugs, punishment for failing to pay one's debts, and general disputes over drugs or drug paraphernalia—all are common to the drug culture," [26] says Gilda Berger, author of *Violence and Drugs.*

From being a drug user, the step to becoming a drug loser is an easy one. Lured by the "easy" and big money involved, kids as young as nine and ten are recruited in the inner cities as lookouts. "For this, they can make up to $100 a day and be rewarded with a pair of fashionable sneakers, a bomber jacket, or a bicycle," [27] says Berger.

The easy accessibility of guns has had an effect
on the incidence of violent crime.

Harry Hamilton, as chief investigator at the Detroit morgue, says: "Kids can make $900 a week standing on a street corner whistling when a scout car goes by. There are plenty of fifteen- and sixteen-year olds doing things like that, but they never get to be twenty-one."[28]

Drug work not only promises ghetto children a fat wallet but it also provides status, risks and thrills, and the opportunity to work their way up into higher-paying drug positions.

From lookouts, young teens can be promoted to "runners," making $300 a day by carrying cocaine and crack around the city. Then, if the youths aren't shot or locked up, they may score big by becoming dealers earning some $3,000 a day.

If caught, juveniles—those under age sixteen—can easily slip through the cracks of the juvenile justice system and be back out on the streets within hours or days.

The rising use of crack has made the problems much worse. Crack, a cheap, smokable form of cocaine, is thought to be one of the most powerful addictive drugs known. As Commissioner of the Nassau County (New York State) Department of Drug and Alcohol Addiction, Harold Adams says, "In all my years of experience, I've never seen a drug that's more frightening and more of a menace than crack because of the violent reaction and nature of those addicted to the substance."[29] And James Payne, chief of Family Court for New York City's Law Department, reports, "We've had almost a 50 percent increase in drug crime. Crack is the main reason. We are seeing kids as young as ten or eleven. They can make $800 a week. They only stay in school because that's where their constituency [customers] is."[30]

In Los Angeles, crack is blamed for escalating violence to ten times what it used to be.[31] And PCP, or angel dust, is even worse than crack in triggering extremely violent behavior.

The recent upsurge in crack has been getting even more youngsters involved in the drug trade, experts point out. "Crack has changed the role of young teenagers in East Harlem society, giving them more power and putting them under less community control than ever before . . . giving them new and enormous power over the older generation,"[32] said Dr. Ansley Hamid of the John Jay College of Criminal Justice in New York in the *New York Times.*

Recent studies have also highlighted that crack can stifle the parental instinct. In other words, when parents become addicted, their crack addiction becomes the most important thing to them, and parenting falls to a much lower priority. The result, experts fear, is that an entire underclass of children is being born not only impaired by drugs but also neglected by addicted parents. The cost to society is enormous, both financially and socially, as these children grow up on the streets with few resources and no one to care about them.

The drug culture has also given rise to more and more street gangs, which pit themselves against each other in territory and status wars.

Alcohol is also a big factor in crime and violence. It not only plays a major role in child abuse and family violence, but is involved in some 65 percent of all homicides every year in the U.S.[33] Excessive drinking not only eases people's inhibitions but is thought to make them more likely to commit violent acts such as robbery, burglary, muggings, and rape. Furthermore, alcohol has been linked to delinquency and crimes of vengeance and passion in a number of studies.

Experts agree that the mix of youth with guns and drugs, worsened by the desperation of poverty, is a lethal one, a blend so toxic that it is killing thousands of young men and women and thousands of innocent bystanders. In the next chapter, we'll see why our justice system fails to bring the growing wave of teen violence to a halt.

8

JUVENILE JUSTICE OR JUVENILE JOKE?

The juvenile justice system is a special failure. Designed to provide a second chance for "juvenile delinquents" who stole hubcaps or picked pockets a generation ago, it gives a third or fourth chance to a whole brand of young thugs for whom the term delinquent is a pitifully inadequate euphemism [a nice way to say something harsh].[1]
—Mortimer B. Zuckerman,
Editor-in-Chief
U.S. News & World Report

Ironically, the juvenile justice system, which was designed to protect children who were thought to be too young to be really bad, has become a big part of the problem in dealing with teen violence. Experts agree that the system is ineffective, inefficient, and totally outdated. Put simply, it has "lost the capacity to punish swiftly and severely."[2]

Originally, the U.S. juvenile justice system set out to protect the immature from being branded their whole lives for a foolish crime. It viewed violent teenagers as children who happened to commit crimes rather than criminals who happened to be young. The system was set up to treat or rehabilitate teenage criminals rather than punish them.

But such a system makes little impact on the new breed of streetwise teen thugs. Many kids who commit crimes know all too well that the system will not do much to them. The first few times they get caught, the system just spits them back out onto the street in no time. If the offender does get put away, it's rarely for very long.

"Small wonder that hardened juveniles laugh, scratch, yawn, mug and even fall asleep while their crimes are revealed in court,"[3] *Time* magazine said.

If twelve years old or younger, child offenders are considered juvenile delinquents. This means that they can only be tried in Family Court, rather than Criminal Court. Regardless of how horrible a crime was committed, a child under thirteen years of age can receive no more than eighteen months' placement in a youth facility, unless he or she has already committed two prior and very serious crimes.

Teenagers thirteen to sixteen are considered "juvenile offenders" rather than criminals, even if they rob, shoot, rape, or murder. These lawbreakers are rarely photographed or fingerprinted and, as recently as 1992, their police records were kept secret and later destroyed so no criminal record would trail them into adulthood. Now, the FBI may collect and distribute state files, that include fingerprints and arrest and conviction records of juvenile offenders charged with serious crimes. Nevertheless, most juvenile hearings are still private and their sentences lenient although they might have committed as many as 100 crimes as a juvenile. In New York State, for example, juvenile offenders can be held in state custody for only eighteen months, unless they have committed the most violent crimes. Most convicted youths, however, are back on the streets in less than four months.

In most states, teens must be either sixteen or eighteen years old to be tried as adults in Criminal Court, regardless of their crimes. Recently, some states changed their laws to allow adult trials for certain youths who commit serious felonies and murder.[4] Otherwise, juvenile offenders go to Family Court, known as "Kiddie Court" on the street. In some states, juries may be requested for more serious offenders.

Every year, some 2.2 million juveniles are arrested; about half are immediately released. Half of those remaining are released shortly after because of inadequate evidence. That means that right off, about 80 percent of teen criminals are back on the streets soon after being arrested.[5]

Of the ones who do go on to court, about 70 percent are first-time offenders and are usually given suspended sentences, put on probation, scolded, and then released. When on probation, the youth is supposed to be monitored closely for any misdeeds. Yet probation officers have huge caseloads and rarely have the time to give much attention to any one case. As a result, youths on probation are frequently unsupervised.

If convicted of a serious crime, a youth usually faces a much more lenient sentence than if he were an adult; murderers may get sent to prison, but usually for only several years. Once released, about 70 percent of offenders go on to commit crimes again.[6] In Philadelphia, for example, two-thirds of violent crimes are committed by just 7 percent of the criminals. By age 18, chronic offenders have more than five arrests, and experts believe they have probably committed dozens more crimes. By age 20, the chronic offenders are committing some 150 crimes a year.[7]

In many cities, however, the justice system is so overworked that criminal youths frequently get off. In New York City, for example, where juvenile criminal cases almost doubled between 1986 and 1989—up to 14,000 cases in 1989—42 percent of the cases didn't

A judge passes sentence on a youthful
offender, shown with his parents.

even get prosecuted, including almost all misdemeanors and even some robberies and assaults. Worse yet, probation officers, each of whom can be expected to keep track of some thirty persons on probation, are severely overloaded in many cities—in San Diego and New York, for instance, caseloads are up to 700 and 800 probationers; in Los Angeles, officers have some 1,000 criminals in their caseload.[8]

"What we are doing is advertising that you can get away with some crimes,"[9] said the chairman of the Committee on Governmental Operations in New York.

States vary widely in how they treat juveniles. Some states only lock up the most violent cases, while others, such as California, crack down with "get tough, lock 'em up" policies. As a result, California locks up a larger percentage of juveniles than any other state.

Across the country, about 83,400 juveniles are in long-term juvenile facilities, and about 2 million are in adult prisons and jails. "Get tough" policies may be getting violent kids off the streets and showing them that the justice system means business, but taxpayers are paying the toll. To keep a juvenile in a state-run reform school costs more than $25,000 a year. That's more than a year's tuition at the most elite colleges.[10]

Worse yet, taxpayers don't seem to be getting their money's worth. Upon release, most juveniles return to crime: almost half of those locked up in 1987 had been arrested more than six times. Experts fear that "many juvenile corrections facilities risk becoming little more than training schools for professional criminals."[11] When juveniles are locked up in places where other people are more violent, they often come out more violent than they went in.

Some states, including Massachusetts, Florida, Utah, and Texas, have opted to either close their juvenile facilities or use them only as a last resort. These states send most teen criminals back home or to special community-based group homes.

Some alternatives for less violent teen criminals include the following:

- Group homes, where youths live with around-the-clock adult supervision; counseling, educational, and recreational opportunities are offered
- Foster care for teens who authorities believe would benefit most from a stable home environment
- Wilderness programs, such as Outward Bound, to strengthen self-confidence and the ability to work well with others
- Close supervision with the child remaining at home; a probation officer or a trained professional monitors the teen's progress
- Family Court community aide programs that offer counseling and liaisons with neighborhood resources
- Family crisis counseling programs that provide "emergency" professional help for the youngsters and their family
- Proctor programs, in which youths live with a proctor until they make satisfactory progress and learn to cope with life in law-abiding ways [12]

These trends are proving to be an "unqualified success," [13] says the National Council on Crime and Delinquency. Its studies report that the rates of recidivism (returning to crime and jail) and of juvenile crime in Massachusetts and Utah for example, have fallen sharply. Opponents say that it's still too early to know for sure whether these options will work in the long run.

While some of the less violent teens are getting unique opportunities to tap into counseling and educational programs, the most violent teens can now be put to death. Murderers as young as sixteen may be executed in states with death penalties, according to a July 1989 Supreme Court decision. Although few are actu-

9

TEEN CRIME AGAINST THE FAMILY

Lizzie Borden took an ax and gave her father forty whacks.
When the job was neatly done, she gave her mother forty-one.

—Unknown

- The night before William Shrubsall was to graduate with honors as his high school's class valedictorian, he beat his mother to death with a baseball bat. He was sentenced to five to fifteen years in prison. The defense attorney pointed to years of alleged physical and emotional abuse of William by his mother.
- Since Cheryl Pierson was eleven years old, her father had been sexually abusing her. Pierson reportedly was forcing the high school cheerleader to have sex with him as often as three times a day. He even molested her on the way to the hospital where her mother lay dying. Once, after she received a valentine from a boyfriend, Pierson gave her a black eye. At eighteen, Cheryl allegedly began to fear that her father would start molesting her eight-year-old

sister, and hired a classmate to gun him down. Pierson, forty-two, was then murdered by the young hit man.

- Two brothers, ages nineteen and twenty-two, were accused of slaying their millionaire parents as the couple watched TV in their $5 million Beverly Hills mansion. The nineteen-year-old, Eric Menendez, a tennis pro, had previously coauthored a screenplay about a son who murders his wealthy parents. Eric's mother had helped her son type the manuscript. The boys testified to years of abuse by their father. Authorities say that the boys stood to inherit more than $10 million. In 1994, both boys' trials ended in hung juries (juries couldn't agree) and mistrials.

- Ever since Richard and Debbie could remember, their father had been beating Richard and sexually assaulting Debbie. They pleaded with their mother to help, but she didn't. Richard went to the authorities, but they decided that abuse could not be too serious in such a nice house. One night, Debbie, seventeen, and Richard, sixteen, prepared. They put the pets in the basement for safekeeping. Debbie stood guard with an M-16 rifle in the living room, while Richard sported a 12-gauge shotgun in the garage. When their father's car pulled up, Richard shot him three times, killing him. "I didn't want to do it," said the boy. "I wanted to drop the gun and hug him." But Richard had tried that before. His father had called him a baby—and beat him all the harder. So he pulled the trigger.[1]

We've already seen in Chapter Five how widespread physical abuse, neglect, and sexual abuse of children are throughout the nation. Experts say that violence at home occurs in about half the families in the U.S.

But children abuse parents, too. One study in the early 1980s indicated that almost 10 percent of American children attack their parents at least once a year.[2]

A 1980 U.S. Department of Justice survey revealed that about 15,730 violent acts are committed by children against their parents annually.[3] Of those attacks, some are deadly: every year about 300 children or teens murder a parent.[4]

Family crises—severe financial, emotional, or health problems—seem to be linked to abuse of parents. As parents seem to lose control, a child is more able to seize control. Sometimes, an older child will beat a parent to punish him or her for drinking too much, or for abusing drugs again, or for being irresponsible in some other way. Violent behavior may also stem from intense dislike of a stepparent or a parent's girlfriend or boyfriend.

When it comes to parent abuse, boys tend to be only slightly more violent than girls. In the vast majority of parent abuse cases, the attackers grew up in families where violent behavior occurred regularly.[5]

"Invariably in the cases that I've worked with, the violence against a parent or against another sibling was violence that grew out of violence toward the child himself," says Ronald Ebert, Ph.D., of McLean Hospital in Belmont, Massachusetts. "That is, the child had been victimized, at least phychologically, often physically, and frequently, sexually."[6]

When children are abused, some grow up passive, depressed, and ashamed. They try to cope with the emotional scars of such abuse for the rest of their lives. Others, as we've seen, learn to respond violently when angry and frustrated. As a result, they end up taking their anger and rage out on others. Still others take abuse for years, but inside, they seethe in rage. One day, these children explode and attack a parent.

Although some teenagers may regularly punch or act out their anger physically toward a parent, most who actually kill a parent never show aggression until the day they lose control. As opposed to "career violent offenders"—the teen who regularly gets into trouble,

Cheryl Pierson, who paid a classmate to kill her father because she said he was sexually abusing her, was released from jail after serving three and a half months of a six-month sentence.

some of it violent—the youth who explodes against a family member is typically meek and obedient for years. Sociologist Clemens Bartollas says:

> Meanwhile, their aggression builds up until their controls can no longer override it, and when they finally explode, they release all of their pent-up anger. The model youth becomes a murderer, perhaps shooting or knifing the victim repeatedly or dismembering the victim. Typically, following the release of their repressed anger, these youths immediately revert to their passive state.[7]

This act of violence is their first, and because it is aimed at the one who caused so much harm, it typically is also their last. While most violent teen criminals have histories of aggression and violence, less than 10 percent of youths who commit parricide—the murdering of a parent—have any kind of previous police record.[8]

When it comes to parricide, boys kill directly, while girls almost never commit the murder themselves. Instead, they hire someone to do it for them. Boys typically kill to "protect" their mothers and siblings (brothers or sisters) from an abusive father. Girls, on the other hand, often kill because they are victims of sexual abuse by fathers. Parricide is almost always premeditated (planned in advance).

In studies that looked at adolescents who committed parricide, researchers have found persistent patterns of chaos and abuse in the family. In fact, more than 90 percent of children who kill a parent have been victims of parental physical, sexual, and mental abuse.[9]

Typically, a parent-killer comes from a family in which extreme violence among family members is common. The child or teen also tends to be isolated from outside sources of help. As the child reaches adolescence, the growing rage inside one day bursts forth and he or she shoots or otherwise attacks a parent.[10] Whereas many severely abused children just bear the scars of their abuse, others retaliate violently one day when the opportunity presents itself. Most children who kill or try to kill a parent are also suicidal. Within six months of the murder, many parent-killers attempt suicide.

PENALTIES

Most states allow youths to be tried as adults when they commit murder, but sentences vary widely. Cheryl Pierson, who hired a schoolmate to kill her father (see the beginning of this chapter), was sentenced to six months in jail and five years' probation. The youth who did the killing was sentenced to eight to twenty-four years in prison. Some authorities fear that light sentences for youths who kill a parent may send the wrong message to other youngsters who dream about revenge. Other people fear that some minors will falsely claim they were severely abused to justify the killing of a parent.

WHAT TO DO

If it is true that violence breeds violence, and that violence *by* parents is the root cause of violence *against* parents (that is, parent abuse and parricide), then the obvious solution is the find ways to reduce violence in the family and the culture at large. We'll examine some of these strategies in Chapter Fifteen.

10

SCHOOL VIOLENCE

Sending your child to school is the most dangerous thing you can ask him to do.
—Mary Lou Guillen Fuller,
New York City mother

- In DeKalb, Missouri, Nathan Faris, age twelve, was angry because a boy teased him for being fat. The next day, Nathan brought in his dad's forty-five semi-automatic to seek revenge. When a thirteen-year-old classmate tried to protect the intended victim, Faris accidentally shot him. Faris then turned the gun to his own head and pulled the trigger.
- In the lunchroom at P.S. 93 in New York City where kindergarteners were eating, a teacher was told that "Melvin has a toy." Toys aren't allowed in the lunchroom, so the teacher went to speak to Melvin. The five-year-old whipped out his "toy" and pointed it at the teacher's chest. It was a loaded and cocked "Saturday-night special."
- In Los Angeles, about 100 children were kept home from high school for months because of the constant

"terrorist" conditions there. Gangs reportedly threatened children with guns and knives in school as well as before and after school.

- Near Washington, D.C., in Fairfax County, Virginia, one of the most affluent districts in the country, violence and weapons in schools have become such a problem that drug-sniffing dogs and metal detectors are used to check kids on their way into school.

In the "good old days" of hoodlums and street toughs, about the worst thing the worst kid in school did was to whip out a switchblade poised for action. But times have changed. Today, kids are toting pistols in backpacks. "Hallway disputes that were once settled with fists or the flashing of a knife blade end in a burst of firepower and a bloody corpse,"[1] reports *Newsweek.*

Statistics vary widely on school violence. Yet they all portray a serious problem for the nation's 45.5 million public school students:

- According to *U.S. News & World Report,* some 3 million crimes are committed on or near school grounds each year.[2] Each hour, some 2,000 students are physically attacked at school; *each day,* more than 160,000 students cut school out of fear.[3]
- The Office of Juvenile Justice and Delinquency Prevention reported that in 1990, one in five American high school students carried a weapon to school in the past month; one in 20, a gun.[4] A University of Michigan report points out that 9 percent of eighth graders carry a weapon to school at least once a month. Some 270,000 guns are in schools *every day.*[5]
- Almost two-thirds of sixth through twelfth graders say they could get a handgun if they wanted one.[6] Some 40 percent of urban teens, 36 percent of suburban teens, and 43 percent of rural teens say they know

someone who has been killed or hurt by guns.[7]
- Violence increased by 16 percent in New York City schools in just one year.[8]
- Violence doesn't only occur in inner city schools. In a survey of more than 1,200 principals across the nation, 64 percent claimed that violence had increased in their schools in the past five years.[9]
- According to the U.S. Department of Justice, nine out of ten school incidents are never reported.[10]

For many kids today, going to school is an act of courage as the threat of crime looms over them. "I think we've entered an era when kids now play cops and robbers with real, loaded and sophisticated weapons," a Washington, D.C., schoolboard member told the *Washington Post*. "And they're doing it as casually as playacting. It's a very eerie and disturbing atmosphere we're in." [11]

According to a middle-school teacher in the Bronx, New York, "Violence has become an accepted part of the day for the students at this school." [12]

In Washington, D.C., for example, the doors of a junior high are

> *riddled with bullet holes that are the fallout of violence related to drug selling in neighboring buildings. . . . Trying to educate children in the midst of one of Washington's worst cocaine and crack markets is wreaking incredible terror in parents, children and teachers. . . . What about the youngsters who . . . day after day . . . watch the body bags being dragged out by police as they try to concentrate on English or algebra?* [13]

Many crimes result from petty hassles—arguments over a cafeteria seat, over a stare, a girl, the taking of a trendy jacket or even a pair of athletic shoes. Sometimes, these conflicts result in death. "[T]he fashion competition among even pre-teenage children on Chicago's grim West Side is not just fierce, it's murderous,"[14] reports *Time*.

The rising tide of violence in schools is, however, mostly blamed on the general increase in drug use and violence on the streets. "We're dealing with all the malaise of society," said a longtime principal at Park West High School in the New York City borough of Manhattan. "The school is a microcosm [tiny world] of society."[15] At Park West, some teachers report that the majority of kids bring weapons to school, many with their parents' encouragement.

"For many youths today, there is no distinction between the school and the street," says Edward Muir, a United Federation of Teachers expert on school security. "Nothing the system can do can totally block out the problems in society."[16]

Some kids bring weapons to school for protection: "You gotta be prepared—people shoot you for your coat, your rings, chains, anything,"[17] a fifteen-year-old junior-high school student in Baltimore told *Newsweek*. He proudly showed the reporter his .25-caliber Beretta.

Other teens believe that a sleek handgun is a status symbol and that flaunting it is a quick ticket to respect. "It's mostly to show off. They think it's the best way to get respect—with a gun, nobody messes with them,"[18] a Washington, D.C., student told the *Washington Post*. For others, a gun is the obvious and acceptable way to resolve a conflict.

As a result, kids are scared to go to school, and it's no wonder. The most dangerous part of the day in many cities is traveling the route between home and school. Drug dealers, gangs, and kids sporting guns and looking for trouble may be lurking around any corner. In some areas of New York City, packs of youths roam from school to school, preying upon students to rob them.

"We're under siege. The whole system is held hostage by a roving band of crazies who want to cause trouble. It breaks my heart to make this an armed camp for my children, who are very good."[19] This was said by a principal at the Bayard Rustin High School for the Humanities in Manhattan. She had to dismiss the students early one day when three carloads of young men descended upon the school, beating up students and security guards.

"The children in this city are in crisis and no one is doing anything about it," said the principal at Boys and Girls High School in Brooklyn, New York. "This city needs to reassure the kids who want to go to school and who want to do what is right."[20]

In Los Angeles, crack is blamed for escalating violence tenfold in communities around the schools.[21] "We're so afraid for our kids," said the mother of a fifteen-year-old boy in the Watts section of Los Angeles. "They are terrorized by kids who are pulling guns inside . . . and outside the class."[22] This woman kept her son home from school for at least two months because of shootings and robberies on the way home from school. On any given day, about 20 percent of the kids at this high school are absent.

Although most of the violence in schools consists of students attacking students, teachers are victims too. In fact, more teachers are being attacked than ever before. From 1973 to 1978, attacks were about 2,850 per 100,000 teachers nationally. From 1979 to 1983, the rate almost doubled. By 1986, 8,000 per 100,000 teachers were being attacked.[23] In New York City, attacks on teachers rose 18 percent between 1988 and 1989.[24]

Each of these attacks resulted in a person getting hurt. A seventh-grade teacher in the Bronx, New York, lost some hearing in both ears after being beaten by students. One elementary school teacher's finger was seriously mangled when a student bit it. Another teacher was hit by a desk. Yet another couldn't use her hand for weeks after a nine-year-old tried to break it.

WHAT TO DO

Until violence is curbed on the streets and in society at large, violence in the schools is going to continue to be a threat to the well-being of students and teachers. But authorities are taking some actions of their own, beefing up security and imposing strict rules on matters ranging from attendance to dress codes. For example:

- In at least forty-five urban centers around the country, metal detectors and/or X ray machines check entering students for weapons.
- Book bags and carrying overcoats, are banned in many areas to prevent students from smuggling in lethal weapons.
- In a small suburb outside Chicago as well as in La Puente, California, parents patrol hallways and stairwells. La Puente reports that crime has fallen by half since 1981, when the patrol began.[25]
- In Greenwood, South Carolina, police officers "adopt" a school, lunching with students and checking school grounds periodically. In Los Angeles, 300 armed police officers do nothing else but patrol the schools at a price tag of $3.3 billion.[26]
- Locker searches are much more common, and in many schools, lockers have been removed so students have no place to hide weapons.
- Many school yards now have tight fences and locked gates.
- To crack down on assaults on teachers, some school districts, such as in New York City, expel students for attacking teachers. Some have also installed panic buttons in classrooms.
- Students are encouraged to leave cash, fancy jew-

More than 400 vials of crack are displayed in a
New York City police station, following the arrest
of an eleven-year-old fifth-grader. Police weren't
certain whether the child was being used as a
courier or whether he just brought the drugs
to school to show them to his friends.

elry, and electronic gadgets at home to prevent robbery temptations.

- To cut down on students' trying to rip trendy high-priced clothes off the backs of others, sometimes killing the victim in the process, schools in Chicago, Baltimore, Detroit, and New Haven, Connecticut, have imposed voluntary or mandatory dress codes of plain clothing.
- To avoid gang conflicts, schools in the Watts section of Los Angeles have banned brown, green, or purple clothes, colored belts or sneakers, hats, bandannas, or braided hair. Such apparel symbolizes certain gangs. The wrong person wearing the wrong color or item might get the wrong guy mad.
- In Los Angeles, where many students are too scared to go to school, districts are setting up classrooms in housing projects. "They're not coming to school, so we'll take the school to the youngsters,"[27] said a deputy superintendent for operations in the Los Angeles school district. In New York City, on the other hand, authorities are designating certain subway cars and buses as student cars and protecting them with police guards on a trial basis.
- Schools and neighborhoods in Chicago have joined forces to form patrols that ensure students safe routes home.
- The American Civil Liberties Union (ACLU), which has long fought with school districts over unlawful student searches, is offering public strategies to curb school violence. It offers tough policies over school absences (truancy), "secret witness" plans in which anonymous tips are encouraged, and educational programs on racism and civil rights, and encourages locker searches when "reasonable suspicion" has been aroused.[28]
- The National School Safety Center at Pepperdine University of Encino, California, has served as a national coordinator since 1984, helping schools rid

To help curb increasing crime in schools,
officials have installed metal detectors—or
security guards or police—to check students
for weapons.

themselves of crime, violence, gangs, bullying, and drugs. NSSC offers technical help, training, and resource materials on how to improve school discipline, attendance, student achievement, and the learning environment.

- Programs such as Cities in Schools, a national partnership between public and private resources, provide extensive social services in schools to kids at risk. A team of counselors keeps close tabs on high-risk students while providing services, from job opportunities and sporting activities to family services, personal living skills, and drug rehabilitation referrals. Such programs have been initiated in more than twenty-five cities, serving more than 18,000 students.

- Violence prevention curricula are sweeping the nation. One program, "Resolving Conflict Creatively," offered in more than 225 schools around the country, trains students to listen carefully, deal with anger and vent it constructively, and overcome racial prejudices and stereotypes. Students learn that conflict is normal, that there need not be a winner or loser, and that they can assert themselves without violence. Some students are trained to become peer mediators, and when a problem arises, the student mediators negotiate with the students in conflict until an agreement is reached.

- Other efforts include: encouraging teachers to refrain from having low expectations of black students, helping principals be strong, preventing schools from getting too large, keeping discipline firm but fair, involving parents more in the school, and fining and expelling students who bring weapons to school.

- School Crime Stoppers (800-245-0009) and WeTip (800-782-7463) are national crime hot lines that offer tips to prevent violence and want reports on school violence.

11

"WILDING" AND MOB VIOLENCE

Said one youth: "When we go wilding, we go beat up somebody."
"Anybody?" asked the interviewer.
"Anybody," he replied.[1]

- In April 1989, a mob of about thirty boys chased down a jogger in New York City's Central Park, viciously beat and raped her, and then left her for dead in the spring mud.
- A few months later, also in New York City, four young black men went to Bensonhurst, a white section of Brooklyn, to check out a used car. Suddenly, they were ambushed by twenty to forty white youths armed with bats. A gunshot rang out and one of the black youths, a sixteen-year-old, fell dead.
- In the winter of 1986, in the Howard Beach section of Queens, in New York City, a group of eleven while youths yelled racial insults at two black men. They beat one and chased the other onto a highway, where he was hit and killed by a passing car.
- Mobs of girls, mostly twelve to fifteen years old,

stormed through Manhattan's well-groomed Upper West Side. On at least forty-five separate occasions, they stabbed innocent passersby—usually white or Asian well-to-do-looking women—with large needles, hatpins, or scissors. One girl told an officer that they attacked "just for the fun of it."[2] Authorities believed most of the attacks were racially motivated.

- In rural Missouri, three teenage boys wondered what it would be like to kill someone. They had become fascinated with death, one reported, through heavy metal music. So out of curiosity, they brutally beat a "friend" to death with baseball bats "because it's fun."[3]

- The annual Labor Day weekend "Greekfest," in which thousands of college fraternity and sorority students descend upon sunny Virginia Beach to party, turned sour in 1989. A mob of 100,000 youths, mostly black college students, according to authorities, clogged the streets, fired shots, and strip-looted about 125 stores. About fifty people were injured and hundreds arrested.

After the above-mentioned notorious attack on a Manhattan investment banker while she jogged in Central Park in April 1989, a new word entered our vocabulary: "wilding." The term describes what some teens do when they roam around together and form "wolf packs," literally going wild: looting, slashing, stabbing, robbing, raping any available "vic" (victim).

Although the term "wilding" is new, the phenomenon is not. Gangs of teenagers, usually boys, have wreaked havoc in groups before. But the attacks have never been quite so savage, so ferocious. And experts grow ever more perplexed because they can't find motives for this vicious behavior.

In New York, where gangs aren't as organized as in cities such as Los Angeles and Chicago, 622 wolf-pack attacks were referred to family court in 1988, up from

602 the year before. Second to crack dealing, such attacks are the most common crime among New York teenagers.[4] Robbery by youth groups has soared 400 percent since 1986.[5]

Philadelphia, too, has its problems, where "packs of youths chant 'Beat, beat, beat' as they roam the streets looking for victims," reports *Time* magazine.[6]

Unlike formal gangs, these kids form packs spontaneously, strike quickly and randomly, and then move on. They roam among victims, schools, and stores, "adding members along the way 'like a pickup game of basketball,' "[7] said one New York City police sergeant.

Many of the packs consist of youths twelve to fifteen years old, although some have kids as young as eight and some have high school youths. When these packs prey on stores, they burst in and overwhelm security guards, go on a wild spree of looting, and then flee. Others rob individuals, beating them up in the process.

What turns a group of teenagers into a savage mob?

The suspected reasons for this kind of wanton, destructive behavior have been discussed previously: alienation, poverty, boredom, rage, weak or abusive families, inequality, violence in television programs and movies, and the erosion of social values.

In New York City, the soaring rate of youthful violent crime goes hand in hand with a 375 percent increase in child abuse and neglect cases since 1984. "Those children are going to become the predators of society,"[8] says a Brooklyn Family Court judge.

Experts state that many of the attacks have their roots in racial hatred. Yet, this doesn't entirely explain the phenomenon because the young attackers often choose victims of the same race.

In the Central Park wilding incident, though experts stressed that anger, poverty, and racism were not necessarily the motives behind the attack. Yet the boys did grow up on the bleaker streets of New York, just blocks from the glittering land of white limousines and mink coats. "They hardly could have reached teen age without realizing and resenting the wide economic and social gap that still separates blacks and whites in this country,"[9] says columnist Tom Wicker.

Scapegoating someone from "the better side of the tracks," someone obviously well-off—a status the youths probably believe they'll never acquire—is often a motive for the wolf-pack attacks, some authorities say. Yet, even some homeless people have been targets of such violence.

A Canadian commentator suggested that these boys grew up having wealth flung in their faces every day, wealth that the boys knew they would never attain. The root of the wilding, he says, may be a result of "those on the bottom end who eventually, not being treated as humans, decide to act as animals."[10]

Boredom and the lack of anything constructive to do have also been cited as causes. Kids hanging around a housing project are apt to want to stir up some excitement. Community and recreational programs are usually scant in the inner city. "These children are bored, looking for stimulation, entertainment,"[11] says a Harvard Medical School psychologist.

Others point to the rituals of adolescence. With peer pressure at an all-time high during adolescence, youths get easily swept up in a mob mentality and then get carried away in its frenzy. No one wants to be the one to hold back and appear to be the coward. Some youths may feel compelled to prove to each other that they're tough.

The type of crowd a teen falls in with can also determine his or her behavior. When someone hangs out with a rough crowd, he's forty times more likely to get into trouble with the law than an equally alienated youth who keeps to himself,[12] according to University of Colorado studies.

When the mob spirit sweeps up individuals, mob

After a young black man was gunned down by
a mob of white youths, blacks demonstrated
for justice. These neighborhood teens
counter demonstrated the demonstration.

psychology tends to wipe out each member's sense of individuality, replacing it with a sense of control, experts say. "Kids who roam in groups gain a sense of power that they do not have individually,"[13] says sociologist Elijah Anderson of the University of Pennsylvania. Youths will do things in groups that they would never do alone.

"It's a little bit like a high on a drug," explains Fred Wright, a psychology professor at the John Jay College of Criminal Justice in New York City. "You feel anonymous because you're in a crowd and nobody sees you. You don't feel individually responsible."[14]

Groups of adolescents are the worst possible combination for trouble, says Dr. Ann Jernberg, director of the Theraplay Institute of Chicago. "The idea of collective violence, the risks involved, is terribly exciting, very dramatic, and sometimes all kids this age need is to see a violent movie or hear a song to encourage them."[15]

These kids feel little remorse, Dr. Jernberg adds, because the mob psychology protects them from feeling directly responsible. As is typical with mobs, the attackers disregard the victim's pain and suffering.

"They don't even see their victim as a victim,"[16] says psychologist Stanton Samenow, a delinquency expert and author of Before It's Too Late: Why Some Kids Get into Trouble.

Usually, kids band together for something to do but with no clear plan in mind. Then, a few boys may start toying with a victim perceived as weak or vulnerable, which makes these boys feel powerful and invulnerable. Some get carried away and get meaner, kicking and beating the victim. Pressured to prove themselves just as savage, other boys in the group start attacking, too. Trying to outdo each other, the violence becomes contagious. Too weak to withdraw, too scared to run, each boy gets caught up in the beating frenzy. One boy, who has been on a number of wilding sprees, says, "After a while, your heart grows cold, but you don't know it yet. [The violence] becomes regular, and you got to push it one step further. You can't be a sucker. You can't be looking back."[17]

If the victim fights back, the attackers become enraged. An experience "wilder," a friend of the Central Park attackers, says that when a victim puts up a fight, the boys will get meaner: "It's their way of showing 'I don't have no feelings, I'm ruthless, I'm a gangster. I'm so cold, I beat that lady up and didn't even care. I'm not scared of anything.' "[18]

Perhaps some boys go wilding to seize control after years of feeling alienated from society, suggests *New York* Magazine. "For a few horrific minutes, the boys who mercilessly pummeled [beat] the jogger, unable to control their own lives, held the power of life and death over someone else."[19]

Being part of such a group is satisfying to some teenagers, giving them a place to belong. "[T]hey can identify with it, they can feel powerful in a world that otherwise makes them feel helpless,"[20] says forensic psychiatrist John Gunn.

There's also little fear of getting caught. As we've seen, if the boys were arrested, their punishment would be endlessly delayed and ridiculously light. "The boys know that; that is one reason they were singing rap songs in their jail cells,"[21] says columnist George F. Will of the boys accused in the Central Part jogger attack.

The Central Park incident was particularly shocking because the attackers seemed to be kids from caring, working-class families. Some commentators said that the only explanation for the savage pack attack was evil. Yet, upon a closer look, the causes behind the wilding violence appear to be the same as the ones we've examined: a complex network of problems stemming from family violence and child abuse, behavior and psychological problems, and neurological problems causing loss of control, learning disabilities, and poor judgment.

The youths in the Central Part wilding attack were not angels before that night. All but one were known trouble-makers in school and to neighbors. At least one had been sexual abused by an acquaintance and physically abused as a small child by his mother; his father was involved in drugs. Another was withdrawn and refused to participate in the most simple school activities; he had been suspended for bringing a knife and Ninja star to school. Another was reared in a home plagued by drugs, drinking, and promiscuity, and he had been suspended from school for fighting.

In other words, all but one of the boys, in fact, had been in serious trouble in school. Several were bullies who terrorized neighbors. The boy's savage behavior, therefore, did not come out of nowhere.

WHAT TO DO

Before mob violence can be curbed among teenagers, the savage streaks in American society will have to be tamed. Often the violence of teenagers is a mirror image of the violence around them—in their families, their communities and culture, and in society at large.

Some programs might help, particularly those that strengthen families plagued by violence, drugs, alcohol, and abuse; and that lure youths off the streets. Whereas recreational and educational opportunities are abundant in affluent suburbs, they're pitifully meager in inner cities. Youths need facilities where they can work out, compete in sports, nurture artistic talents, and interact with positive male role models. Such youths also need positive employment opportunities.

Finally, the court system must change to ensure that teen thugs who prey in packs know that punishment for such behavior will be swift and severe.

12

GANGS

You join to survive. If you're not in a gang, you have no protection from other bangers. Once you're in, though, you're in for good.[1]
—A nineteen-year-old member of the Los Angeles gang, The Crips.

Teenagers have banded together in gangs for years. In the last chapter, we saw how some teens group together on the spur of the moment and go off on wild crime sprees. But in many cities, bands of youths have formed formal gangs with clear ladders of leadership, strict codes of behavior and dress, and sometimes even their own language and hairstyles. What is new and disturbing is the alarming increase in violence and the ever-increasing numbers of casualties these gangs leave in their wake.

In the 1950s and 1960s, gangs were a looming threat, but their activity calmed down in the 1970s. Only Detroit, Chicago, Los Angeles, Boston, Philadelphia, and New York had significant gang problems. But during the 1980s, gang activity gained momentum again. As gangs traded in their chains, knives, and fists for automatic weapons, explosives, and shotguns, and, at the same times, jumped into the drug trade, the danger from gangs posed ever more serious problems. "The influence of drugs and weapons," says Edward Muir, a United Federation of Teachers safety expert, "is something that has really hyped the youth gang danger far out of whatever problems we faced with similar groups in the past. They are becoming a very dangerous threat to society." [2]

Today, the danger from gangs is more serious than at any time since World War II. [3] Many gangs are highly organized units with national operations. They are quick to kill, and the stakes are high: millions of dollars of drug money. A recent trend has been the increase in the numbers of girls joining gangs. Some are all-girl gangs but as girls get tougher, they are accepted more widely into what used to be all-boy gangs. Newsweek reported that some of the girl gangs, such as the two biggest ones in Boston, "are every bit as ruthless as the boys', shooting, stabbing, fighting, and participating in drive-by shootings." [4]

With drug wealth behind many of the gangs, some gang members are traveling to new cities to set up gang and drug operations in new markets. As a result, gangs are sweeping across the nation into smaller cities that never before had gang problems. Seattle; Portland; Atlanta; Miami; Phoenix; Denver; Minneapolis; St. Paul; Evanston, Illinois; Salt Lake City; Riverside, California; and San Diego have all recently reported gang problems. So have New Haven, Connecticut; Jackson, Michigan; Portsmouth, Virginia; Peoria, Illinois; St. Louis; Tallahassee; Baton Rouge; Jackson, Tennessee; Kansas City; and Tulsa. [5]

WHY KIDS JOIN GANGS

Gangs have sprung up in cities where many poor children and young teenagers grow up in decayed slums with little hope for any positive change. These communities are fractured and dirty, strewn with garbage and junkies. The future is bleak. The youths enter adolescence feeling insecure and worthless. Many believe they cannot achieve the status and well-being of middle-class America through legitimate means; they feel deprived.

It's tempting to point to poverty and slums as the root of gangs, since ghetto teens, particularly minorities, make up the majority of gangs. But experts point out that middle-class kids join gangs, too, though their gangs are not as violent.

"[T]he violence of the typical gang is not necessarily linked to poverty but rather to gaining 'respect,' " says William Sanders, an expert on juvenile delinquency. It's the thirst for status, he says, that attracts kids to gangs, which bestow status. It gives a youth a "reputation," a chance "to be somebody."

"A boy can be a 'man' among his peers and someone who is 'taken seriously,' aspects of identity for juveniles that are denied in larger society,"[6] says Sanders.

As the traditional supports of home, school and community have broken down for many youths, gangs provide teens with a place to belong and share an identity with peers. Fearful of gangs, many youths are lured into them to become part of the "in group" and to feel protected. To not join the gang could mean being vulnerable to gang harassment.

Many youths are proud to be part of a gang. Some gangs provide "macho" images for their members, a source of support, a sort of family. Often, youths admire older gang members, viewing them as heroes and role models. Belonging to a gang makes youths feel valued and important. Gangs also provide a source of thrills; they give teens a group of peers to take chances with, to stir up some excitement with. Gangs can provide a source of strength and power to teens who feel worthless and insecure. "Gangs allow even the most cowardly and impotent to feel brave and powerful,"[7] reports *Time*.

But for many teens, gang membership means a ticket to quick and "easy" money, an opportunity for wealth through illegal means. Many gang members have given up on the "American dream," believing that the conventional route to success (good education, good jobs) is not available to them; they feel they need to take what opportunities they can. Says a Los Angeles prosecutor who volunteers in Los Angeles schools: "The kids that are selling crack when they're in the fifth grade are not the dumb kids. . . . They're the ambitious kids . . . trying to climb up their own corporate ladder. And the only corporate ladder they see has to do with gangs and drugs."[8]

GANG ACTIVITY

Although some gangs are harmless groups of teens that provide their members with a sense of belonging and security, research shows that individuals in gangs commit much more violence that those out on their own. One Harvard expert, for example, claims that more than 70 percent of serious juvenile crime is committed by gangs.[9]

The most menacing gangs deal in drugs. The lure for a teen is almost irresistible—a fourteen- or fifteen-year-old can make about $600 a day delivering drugs.

"It's hard to tell a fifteen-year-old with $3,000 in his pocket, who before never had a dollar, that this is the wrong way to go," says a Los Angeles police detective with the antigang unit.[10]

Most often, gang violence stems from fights over turf and drug clients and attempts to wipe out rivals, punish informers, and hurt those who don't pay their drug bills or who steal, cheat, or lie to other gang members.

Social and sports programs that give young people a place to meet in the evening can provide an alternative to the violent youth gangs that lonely, alienated teens join.

WHO AND WHERE ARE THE GANGS?

Some of the most powerful and threatening gangs are in Los Angeles and Chicago. No less sinister are the Skinheads, who are scattered across the nation in an informal network of gangs.

Los Angeles

There are probably more gangs and gang members in Los Angeles than anywhere else in the country. Estimates range from 450 to 800 gangs[11] in the city, with 150,000 known gang members altogether.[12] Experts estimate that about 35 percent of the city's gang members are juveniles. Although most gang members are blacks or Hispanics, some are Asians, Samoans, or whites.[13] The Crips (whose name comes from "crippling") is the largest and oldest gang. It's a black gang with subgroups all over the city. Crips not only feud with other Crips gangs, but ferociously fight over turf and drug customers with their arch rivals, a gang called the Bloods.

These gangs have a strong subculture of their own, with secret hand signals, strict uniforms, and codes of behavior. The Crips wear short pigtails and blue on everything, from shoelaces to bandannas. The Bloods wear red on everything.

So many gangs square off in Los Angeles, each with its own dress code, that one school that covers territories claimed by at least six gangs has had to ban its students from wearing brown, green, and purple clothing altogether, as well as colored belts or sneakers, bandannas or braided hair.[14]

In 1987, almost 600 people, among them many innocent victims, were killed in gang cross fire.[15] "The scope of the gang problem in this city and county is horrendous,"[16] said the assistant chief of Los Angeles's school police department.

As these gangs have reaped drug riches, their leaders from L.A. are believed to be the ones fanning out to other cities, setting up drug markets, "McDonald's-like franchises,"[17] in San Diego; San Francisco; Portland; Seattle; Phoenix; Tucson; Shreveport, Louisiana; and Toronto, Canada.

Chicago

Chicago reports about 125 gangs with 15,000 members all told. The Black Gangster Disciples is perhaps the most organized. These gang members infiltrate housing projects, forcing tenants out and setting up their own "private fortresses."[18]

"Gangs have so worked their way into the fabric of the community that no one—the police, the housing authority or the tenants—is certain how to get rid of them,"[19] reports the *Wall Street Journal*.

They take over buildings, terrorize neighbors, and swiftly execute anyone who reports them to the police or testifies against them.

Gang leaders recruit youngsters as young as eight and ten, luring them with jogging suits and "ghetto blasters." In exchange, the youths run drugs for older members.

Detroit

Although the mayor of Detroit insists that his city no longer has a gang problem now that the leaders have been jailed, new evidence reveals that several large youth gangs are raking in millions of dollars by working secretly and "under cover." The Young Boys Inc. and the Pony Down gangs reportedly have powerful drug empires that not only lure ghetto youths but, increasingly, teens from middle-class neighborhoods who are drawn by the quick money.

Skinheads

As young as eleven and usually no older than their early twenties, these snarling teenagers have formed an informal network of racist gangs.

Their look: shaved heads or closely cropped hair, combat boots, black leather or military jackets, and tatoos of dragons, eagles, "Skinhead," and satanic symbols. Their pet peeves: "peace punks," homosexuals, and liberals. Their passion: the hard-pounding, white-power music called "Oi!" that glorifies working-class values and white-power idealism.

Many skinheads are not racist or violent but just adopt the look and music of the Skinhead culture. Others embrace the white pride themes but don't attack minorities. The most menacing members of the Skinhead culture, however, are the ones quick to express their hate.

Their slogans: *"Get Out!* Filthy Jew *Pigs!"*; "Trash 'em! Smash 'em! Make 'em die!"

Skinhead groups, with names such as the Bashboys, the Death Squad Skins, the War Skins, and the Reich Skins, not only sport knives, baseball bats, chains, and Doc Maarten steel-toed boots to do their bashing but also handguns, sawed-off shotguns, and semiautomatics. Proud of their snarling image, members tattoo swastikas, death heads, Iron Crosses, and other violent images on their knuckles, down their legs, up their arms, and even across their upper lips.

Organizations that monitor hate groups report that skinheads are responsible for at least 1,500 incidents of unprovoked attacks, including vandalism, beatings, and murder.[20]

Skinheads have been on a rampage of racist violence, beating, bashing, stabbing, and shooting blacks and other minorities around the country. In 1986, the

"Skinhead Nation" was a scant 300 young people; by fall of 1988, 2,000 skinheads were reported in twenty-one states. By 1993, reports put the count at 3,500 skinheads in thirty-one states.[21]

As their numbers have swelled, so have their violent racist crimes. Crimes against Jews, for example, were reported at their highest rate ever since record-keeping statistics began. In 1989, skinhead attacks against Jews soared 180 percent from the previous year: 116 incidents in twenty-four states.[22] In 1990, the Anti-Defamation League of B'nai B'rith also reported an upsurge of racist crimes by skinheads in schools.

Although the largest concentration of skins is in the West, the most recent wave of recruitment comes out of the Southeast.

Perhaps most troubling about the skinheads is their recruitment by neo-Nazi and Ku Klux Klan groups, including the White Aryan Resistance, the White Student Union, the Aryan Nations, and Klan groups in at least seven states.[23] All of these groups preach white supremacy and hatred against those who aren't pure white Aryans. Members of these groups are notorious for committing violent crimes against minorities.

The recruitment of skinheads by these white supremacists has many Klan watchers alarmed. They fear the new alliances may breathe renewed life into the wilting white supremacist movements, thereby posing a much more dangerous threat to society. The aging white supremacists give the skinheads recognition, a cause, a philosophy, and a sense of importance. In return, the skins could give the sagging white-supremacist movement a fresh start with the skinheads' violent streak, anger, and youthful vigor. At the same time, skinhead groups in Europe have been gaining force, and some people fear that it is just a matter of time before all the groups join hands in their hate war.

WHAT TO DO

Authorities have been trying to fight gangs for a long time. Here are some of their strategies:

- Cracking down. In 1988, Los Angeles police swept through their city, arresting 800 gang members, in the hope that such a crackdown would intimidate gangs and reduce their activities. Unfortunately, the plan backfired: the mass arrests ended in mass dismissals. The thugs came home heroes, having faced the enemy and returned victorious. ID jail bracelets and clothing stamped "L.A. County jail" "earn[ed] high fashion marks . . . bedazzl[ing] younger onlookers." [24]

- Outreach programs. Involving parents, teachers, and other community members, these programs help provide summer jobs as well as other services to help teens adapt to more conventional life-styles. "These are the children of people who live in the community. They are not monsters," sociologist Joan Moore, who has been working with Los Angeles gangs for more than a decade, told the *Christian Science Monitor:* "The difference between a gang and a group of kids on the street corner is often very small." [25] Moore believes that such programs could keep the kids from joining or forming menacing gangs.

- After-school resources. Irving Spergel, a professor at the University of Chicago, has a three-year grant from the Office of Juvenile Justice and Delinquency Prevention, to develop model approaches to combat gangs. To target teens about to get involved in gang activity, he says that after-school programs are essential. Ideally, the programs must coordinate the youths, their homes, community agencies, and the police.[26]

- Intervention networks. Already in place in Chicago, a twenty-four-hour telephone hot line dispatches specialized professionals to intervene at the scene of gang incidents. The intervention network in Chicago also includes "attitudinal development" classes for gang members still in school and coordinates parent patrols to ensure that students have a safe route to get home. The network also works with many other agencies for special referrals, and with elementary schools to address the gang problem.

  In Philadelphia, the Crisis Intervention Network is said to have had "phenomenal success" and is now being used in other cities too.[27] Hot lines dispatch intervention workers to trouble spots, and workers use dispute-resolution and rumor-control techniques. Objective measures, however, have never been used to really assess how effective these intervention networks have been.

- Early education. In Los Angeles, a pilot program of fifteen hours of education at the fifth-grade level is being tested to explore issues relating to self-esteem and alternatives to gangs, as well as the drawbacks of belonging to gangs.

- Close monitoring. In come cities, probation officers specialize in gangs. Rather than trying to rehabilitate gang members, these officers intensely monitor gang members on probation and impose stiff penalties for those who violate probation.[28]

- More convictions. In some cities, a program called Operation Hardcore is said to have increased the conviction rate of gang members by employing specialists to work with police officers to build cases against targeted gang leaders.[29]

- Constructive channeling of adolescent energy. Other attempts to try to guide the potentially violent energy of gang members into more constructive activities. Mural projects in Los Angeles started in 1973 and persist today. Some former gang members now wage war with spray paint. They'll ambush buses, tunnels, and billboards, often late at night. Although these gangs and their artistic endeavors are not sanctioned by authorities, their spray-painting does help vent some of the pent-up frustrations youth may feel during adolescence.

It will not be easy to do away with violent gangs. Youths at risk must be identified early and shown better alternatives to gang life. The answers, one again, seem to reside in stronger families, more resources for underprivileged youths, good community alternatives, and brighter opportunities for kids who see very few options in life but to join a gang.

13

SEXUAL VIOLENCE

The rising tide of assaults has created a rippling pool of fear. Some teachers now send little girls to the bathroom in pairs. Young women say they are afraid to take a shower or run the hair dryer; the noise could mask an assailant's approach. At college parties, many coeds clutch their cocktail glasses, worried that knockout drops could be slipped into their drinks.[1]

—Time *magazine*

- In August 1986, two young people went out on a date. Both were children of Manhattan's wealthy elite. But only the dark, handsome young man, Robert Chambers, nineteen, a "preppie," made it home that night. While they had sex that night in New York's Central Park, his date, Jennifer Levin, eighteen, was choked to death. Chambers said it was an accident that occurred during "rough sex."
- In an affluent New Jersey suburb, eight of the most popular and handsome high school athletes lured a

seventeen-year-old mentally impaired girl down to a basement. Some of the boys gang-raped her while others watched. For months they bragged about the assault in school. Police finally took some action three months later. (See Chapter One for more details.)

- In Los Angeles, a twelve-year-old girl was abducted and sexually attacked for four days by dozens of teen boys—all members of the Rolling 40s Crips gang.
- In Columbia, South Carolina, two boys aged thirteen and fourteen raped an eleven-year-old girl in school.
- In Detroit, an eleven-year-old boy joined a friend in raping a two-year-old girl. The boys tossed the girl into a garbage dumpster when they were finished.

Teenage boys are sexually attacking females more than ever before. The attackers come from all races and socioeconomic classes. Arrests of boys aged eighteen and under for rape and sexual assault have more than doubled since 1976.[2] Between 1983 and 1987 alone, these arrests jumped 15 percent, while the population of this age group went down 2 percent,[3] according to the FBI.

All told, adolescents are arrested for about 15 percent of the rapes in this country.[4] These numbers only reflect the attacks that are reported to the police. Experts estimate the real incidence of these crimes is *ten* times the reported rate.

Teenagers and young adults, aged fifteen to twenty-four, are not only the most likely age group to rape but also to be raped. About one of every four rape victims is a teenage girl.[5] Nine times out of ten, the teen victim knows her attacker.[6] Frequently, the attackers are well liked and well respected in their communities.

Date rape, or acquaintance rape, is one of the most common sexual crimes committed by teenagers. According to recent surveys, about one in five young

Two Glen Ridge, New Jersey, high school students defend their eight classmates who were accused of sexually assaulting a seventeen-year-old mentally impaired girl.

women will have been forced to have sex by the time she is college age.[7] Yet, less than 1 percent of these rapes will be reported, leaving the attacker free to commit the crime again and again.[8] About half the college men and about 40 percent of the college women surveyed admitted that there are some circumstances under which they thought it was okay to force a young woman to have sexual intercourse.[9]

Violence in teenage dating relationships is also surprisingly common, although incidence statistics vary widely. Researchers have found evidence of violence in dating relationships in 12 to 67 percent of the relationships.[10]

Just as violence and sex often are linked in television shows and movies, many teens also associate the two. In fact, about one-quarter of victims of date violence and one-third of the aggressors view violence in dating as a sign of love and a natural part of an intimate relationship.[11]

Typically, date violence and acquaintance rape occur on dates or at parties. A typical case is a young woman between fifteen and twenty-four who meets a young man, say at a party. The two have coffee together or later go on a date. When the couple is alone in one of their apartments, the boy initiates sex and the girl may comply up to a certain point. At some point, however, the girl says no but the young man forces her to have sex against her will.

CAUSES OF TEEN SEXUAL VIOLENCE

One reason why young men force young women to have sex with them is that our culture raises males to believe themselves to be strong, powerful, and sexually aggressive. Women are raised to be sexually alluring but, at the same time, to play hard to get and be coy. Generally, girls are also typically more passive and nurturing than boys and less assertive.

When a boy and girl tangle sexually and the girl says no, the male often thinks that the female is just playing hard to get and that she expects and even wants to be convinced or pressured into having sex.

Such behavior patterns set women up to be forced to have sex, says Cornell University's Andrea Parrot, Ph.D., an expert on date rape. Parrot's studies have found that the most likely place for a date rape to occur is in the room or home of either the male or female involved. Alcohol and loud music are also often part of the date rape picture.

Popular culture not only fosters the belief that men should be sexually aggressive and women compliant and willing to give in but also gives teens the impression that everybody is having sex. Further, many TV programs and movies depict women enjoying forced sex. Also, some young men come to believe that they "deserve" sex after taking a girl out and spending money on her.

Young women are not very well prepared to insist upon what they want, leaving them vulnerable to aggressive men. Adolescents are particularly at risk because they are dating at ever younger ages with few restrictions or rules to guide them.

"Many thirteen-year-olds are confronting sexual situations that their parents didn't face until they were twenty years old,"[12] Parrot points out.

Whereas the roots of stranger rape, a much rarer situation, are most commonly power and anger as opposed to sexual gratification, experts believe that when it comes to adolescent rape, most of which is acquaintance rape, sexual pleasure is often a factor. During adolescence, sexual and aggressive impulses are particularly intense. "And many youths are simply socially inept and unable to woo female affection," reported *Time* magazine. "Frustrated, they take what they want."[13]

Yet experts stress that the family and culture, once again, are probably influential in setting the stage for adolescent sexual aggression. About 40 percent of adolescent sex offenders were sexually abused themselves, and 60 percent were physically abused,[14] says Judith Becker, M.D., a psychiatrist at the New York State Psychiatric Center Sexual Behavior Clinic.

Many youths learn at home that victimizing women is a way of life. Not only do they witness it at home but their culture reinforces the same images. "Slasher" movies, so popular with teenagers, commonly portray women being tortured, raped, and murdered.

Some heavy metal and rock music and music videos also may be contributing to the wave of sexual violence among American teenagers. "I'll either break her face or I'll take down her legs, get my ways at will," says a song by Mötley Crüe, "Too Fast for Love." Many other heavy metal songs make similar references.

All these cultural influences that show females as sexual victims not only give youths ideas they may not have had themselves but also may lead them to believe that such behavior is acceptable, perhaps even expected of virile young men. At the same time, some of these media dehumanize women, treating them more like objects than fellow human beings. Movies and rock videos also don't show the victim's pain and suffering.

All these factors contribute to "an infectious malaise that not only enables attackers to do as they will but also allows bystanders to watch and do nothing, and still others to hear of brutalities and not be horrified,"[15] reports *Time* magazine.

Further, the crack epidemic may be contributing to sexual violence, because the drug tends to leave users sexually aroused. When crack users don't have a willing partner, experts point out, they may be tempted to rape.

GANG RAPES

The forces behind gang rapes are much like those behind wilding. Typically, one member of the group triggers the attack, and the assault escalates as members of the group try to outdo each other and prove themselves as "men." Soon, the group gets caught up in the frenzy of the attack.

Gang rapers not only try to prove to each other how macho or brutal they are, but, as in wilding incidents, they may be trying to prove to themselves how they can seize control in a world where they believe they have little control.

As with wilding, members of a gang in an attack feel more anonymous in a group and less responsible for the group's deeds. As the teens try to prove their masculinity to each other and their powerfulness, the individuals end up doing things they never would imagine doing by themselves.

WHAT TO DO

The following are some ways to curb sexual violence by teenagers.

The glorification of sex and violence in movies, music, and videos must be reduced. Six states are currently considering laws that would require warning labels on rock albums with violent / sexual lyrics. Citizens concerned about violence and sex in the media have formed organizations such as Americans for Responsible Television to monitor and try to pressure individuals in the fields of television, movies for teens, and music to reduce the glorification of sex and violence.

- Many juvenile offender programs provide teen sex offenders with individual and group therapy as well as regular meetings with victims. The hope is that the offenders, by sitting face-to-face with victims, will better understand the pain and suffering these people endure.

- Sex education classes need to explore the emotional aspects of sex rather than just the physical aspects.
- Young women need to learn how to be more assertive in their communication, insisting on no when they mean it. Many colleges offer rape prevention education and assertiveness training. These programs also point out risk factors such as being alone with a young man before knowing him well, drinking or taking drugs on dates, and giving inconsistent signals with verbal and body messages.

14

KIDS WHO
KILL . . . THEMSELVES

Death is not romantic.
You do not come back and visit.
You do not even a score.
You only take a player out of the game.[1]
—Chicago Sun-Times

Teenagers commit many kinds of violence, but perhaps one of the most lethal is when they turn their anger and hostility inward and commit suicide.

Consider these tragic statistics:

- Over the past two to three decades, teenage suicide attempts have soared between 350 and 700 percent.[2] Every hour about fifty-seven children and adolescents try to kill themselves in the U.S., every day more than 1,000 try,[3] and every year, almost half a million try.

- More than 40 percent of teen girls and 25 percent of teen boys have seriously considered committing suicide. One of every seven teens has tried to kill himself at least once.[4]

- Since 1970, teenage suicides have jumped 300 percent,[5] with suicides among children aged ten to fourteen doubling; more than half of them used a gun.[6]

- Every ninety minutes, an American teenager succeeds in committing suicide.[7] That's an average of eighteen kids a day—a total of 6,500 a year.[8]
- Although girls account for some 90 percent of attempted suicides among teenagers,[9] boys are far more successful in completing the suicide because mor boys use guns. Boys kill themselves at a rate three to four times greater than girls.
- White teenagers kill themselves at a rate five times greater than blacks, while Native Americans kill themselves ten times more often than whites. Rural youths commit suicide at much higher rates than urban youths.[10]
- Suicide is the second leading cause of death among youths.

CAUSES OF TEEN SUICIDE

Without question, teen suicide is soaring. The dismal statistics don't even represent how serious the problem is, because many suicides are disguised. Many car accidents, for example, particularly single-car fatalities, are actually suicides. Some experts estimate that the real rate of youth suicide in this country is more than *four* times the rate illustrated above.

Why are so many teenagers so miserable that they feel that the only way out of their problems is to kill themselves? Because feelings of helplessness and hopelessness, sadness and depression, seem so overwhelming during adolescence. Sometimes depressed people are withdrawn and passive; sometimes the depressed person will eat too much or too little, abuse drugs or alcohol, get pregnant, or start failing in school.

Such depressions are often triggered by loss: loss of a parent, friend, or romance; loss of the feeling that the

Teenagers live in a very stressful, highly pressured environment. Some of them view suicide as the only way out of what is a life without hope.

person is in control; failure in school or sports; loss of the feeling that one is worthy; loss of a sense of meaning in life. Sometimes, depressions are caused by biochemical problems in the brain.

Depressed teens most at risk for killing themselves have histories of antisocial behavior, of serious problems at home, and / or of abusing drugs or alcohol. In fact, teens taking drugs, including alcohol, have been found to have three times the rate of attempting suicide than non-substance users.

American teenagers live in a stressful, competitive society. Divorce is breaking families up. Families are suffering serious economic problems. Many move often, interfering with the formation of important and lasting social bonds with others. Adolescence itself is fraught with anxiety, self-doubt, and fear of failure (see Chapter Four). At the same time, teens are undergoing major and confusing physical and emotional changes.

Amidst teens' personal confusion in a confusing society, they are exposed to violence and suicide in their music and culture. Some suicides, in fact, have been blamed on depression aggravated by heavy metal music with suicidal lyrics. One California nineteen-year-old was wearing headphones and listening to Ozzy Osbourne's "Suicide Solution" when he killed himself. Another youth, a sixteen-year-old, was listening to AC/DC's "Highway to Hell" when he hanged himself.

Teen suicide cuts across all socioeconomic lines. Both poor and privileged teens kill themselves. Some well-off communities have experienced waves of suicides and copycat suicides. During 1983 and 1984, one Texas community lost eight teenagers over a period of fifteen months; another lost six youths in two months. After four teens killed themselves with gas fumes in a car garage in New Jersey in 1987, two Illinois teenagers copied the suicide several days later. In

1985, after all three networks showed movies about teen suicide in Dallas, the city lost twenty-five teenagers to suicide in the following months.

Several studies have revealed that media attention to suicides in movies or the news is linked to a boost in teenage suicide attempts. One reason may be that such reports may bring thoughts of suicide to the surface in the teens who watch them and may, in a way, give them "permission" to do the same.[11]

Suicide experts point to several factors most strongly linked to teen suicide: a breakdown of the family, youth unemployment, suicide by a member of the family, and few, if any, religious ties. Typically, presuicidal teens are either isolated or passive, and they have a chip on their shoulder or have shown aggressive behavior in the past. Suicides have also been strongly linked to histories of physical and sexual abuse.[12]

A suicide attempt is usually a cry for help—a plea for someone to come and pay attention to the deep suffering inside. Rather than thinking about death and its finality, many teenagers get caught up with fantasies about how sorry their families and friends would be if they were to die, romanticizing the funeral and tears of loved ones. Many teens may not really want to die, but desperately want the pain of daily life to go away. For those with poor impulse control, suicide becomes a viable option—especially if the pain caused by emotional, physical, and/or sexual abuse has been constant.

"Kids see that this is a glamorous way to die, a way to get a lot of attention that they couldn't get in life," Pamela Cantor of Harvard Medical School and president of the National Committee for the Prevention of Youth Suicide told *Time*. When a teenager commits suicide and gets all this attention as a result, other kids may be drawn to copying the suicide in their struggle to get such attention, too.[13]

WHAT TO DO

To combat the wave of teen suicide plaguing our country, some communities have tried the following:

- Suicide prevention hotlines where trained counselors are available twenty-four hours a day to talk
- Suicide prevention education for parents, teachers, and youths to help recognize the symptoms in others and to teach teens how to cope with stress and depression using clear communication techniques (since one in about every 110 suicide attempts is fatal, experts stress the need to know how to deal with a depressed and suicidal person) [14]
- Implementing community action teams to prevent copycat suicides after a suicide and to ensure that a suicide does not get glorified attention
- Curbing attention to suicide in television and music

15

WHAT CAN BE DONE?

Regardless of where they live, most youths aren't violent, and given a choice, they would rather not live in a world of guns, drugs and death.[1]
—*Representative George Miller of California, chairman of the House Select Committee on Children, Youth and Families*

Although many experts have offered many solutions, teen violence is a complex problem. As we've seen, it is the result of many factors: child abuse and neglect and other acts of violence in the home; single mothers who have few resources and little knowledge about parenting; children with little family or school support who have low self-esteem, think they're "dumb" and give up on school; poverty-stricken and dangerous neighborhoods with extremely high unemployment rates, where children are exposed to violence almost daily, and hope for a good life is all but extinguished; easily available guns and a drug culture that entices children with its promise of riches; and young people with poor social skills whose anger and frustration too easily results in violence.

To relieve teen violence in our society, these risk factors must be eliminated. Families and communities must be strengthened in order to resist the negative effects of a violent environment, poverty, and discrimination. And waiting until children are adolescents is too late. More and more studies stress that programs have to begin early in childhood to counter the effects of the risk factors known to contribute to aggression. It will not be easy, simple, or cheap. Every segment of society must make a commitment, and the more cooperative each segment is with the others, the more powerful the overall impact will be to reduce violence among our teenagers.

The following is a broad palette of suggestions, starting at the individual and family level and then broadening out to include how the community, educational, and societal and judicial institutions can help reduce teen violence.

Basically, there are two approaches. One is prevention, to intervene early to ensure that the next generation will be less vulnerable to the ravages of family violence, poverty, drugs, and guns. The other approach is to intervene with today's offenders, providing effective drug and alcohol treatment; teaching positive communication, job, and social skills; offering better alternatives to a life on the streets; and making changes in the legal system to hand down consistent, efficient, and stern punishments appropriate to the crime.

PROGRAMS ON THE INDIVIDUAL LEVEL

- Helping unprepared parents become better parents. The links between abuse and delinquency, leading to violence, have been confirmed again and again. Every effort must be made to protect the next generation from suffering at the hands of dysfunctional families. Support and regular visits from trained nurses as well as educational and vocational resources for disadvantaged young mothers and fathers would help curb family violence.

- Early identification. One of the most powerful ways to reduce teen violence is to identify aggressive children *early:* very aggressive boys are three times more likely to become criminals.[2] Parents and teachers must learn to recognize antisocial and/or aggressive children: the ones who refuse to make an effort in school; who get thrills from stealing lunch money, destroying property, and abusing teachers; who don't cooperate and are quick to get into trouble.
- Early intervention. The older the aggressive child, the harder it is to teach him or her alternatives. Yet, here are some approaches that seem to be working:

    Cognitive therapy. So-called antisocial children look at the world differently than others. While still young, these children can be taught an entirely different way of thinking—responsible thinking. Children can be shown how they hurt others, how to evaluate their own behavior, how to control their impulses, how to deal with stress and anxiety, how to resist peer influence, how to ask for help, how to deal with authority figures, and how to make better, more responsible decisions.

    Empathy training. For aggressive youngsters in middle elementary school, for example, programs can help children identify with the feelings of others. Through role playing, a child learns to imagine himself in the place of others. As a result, he becomes less aggressive toward others.[3]

    Pair therapy. By pairing an overly aggressive boy who often can't keep friends with a more passive one, experts have found that the aggressive boy learns totally new approaches in how to get what he wants. Rather than fighting for his desires, he learns to negotiate and bargain. Other experts put one aggressive boy in a group of four. Listening skills and negotiations are taught and then practiced in the group.

Youth facilities for chronic offenders. One rather radical approach is to place the crime-prone child (the one who has committed five or ten crimes by age twelve) in a special residential facility where he earns privileges, is rewarded for honesty and good deeds, and is taught social skills and personal responsibility. Rather than just waiting for such delinquent children to become violent criminals, such a program might intercept the predictable progression from aggressive child to violent criminal.[4]

PARENTS AND FAMILY

Children are taught everything in school, from math to volleyball to cooking, but never do they learn how to perform the most difficult and important jobs of their lives: how to raise and discipline a child when they're adults, teach values, and be positive role models for their children as well as how to get along with others. Poor parenting skills and parent maltreatment of children have been blamed for up to 90 percent of the problems teenagers have with drugs, alcohol, and crime. Experts stress time and again the need for young adults to receive parent training and support.

Parenting Classes

- Rather than resorting to threats, physical and verbal abuse, humiliation, and criticism for unruly children, parents and parents-to-be need to be trained in how to raise responsible children with firm, consistent discipline coupled with love and tenderness. Such training would go far in avoiding family violence and child abuse and combating gangs and other youth crises.

- Parents of wild young boys aged four to nine can be taught a program from the University of South Carolina that helps parents keep a record of their child's specific problems and shows them how to institute a program of rewards and privileges for good behavior and withdrawing such rewards for bad behavior.
- Tough Love, an organization of groups of parents around the country, offers strategies and support to parents with children who are out of control or violent and/or using drugs or alcohol. Parent groups meet weekly to help each other. Tough Love's strategies are controversial because the organization advocates strictness with teens yet claims that it replaces the family and community networks now absent in so many places.

Holding Parents Responsible

California has passed an anti-youth-gang law that allows parents to be arrested for failing to intervene in their teenager's gang activities. Whether such a law will prove constitutional or effective remains to be seen. Yet, experts agree that better and more attentive parenting would greatly reduce teen violence.

THE COMMUNITY

Resources for Parents

To reduce child abuse and family violence, one of the most powerful predictors and causes of violence in teens and adults, families must have access to help.

- Twenty-four-hour hot lines for counseling and advice are available and effective in many communities.
- Family resource centers. In Washington, New York,

and Hartford, Connecticut, for example, such programs connect highly stressed families with a "mentor" from a church or community agency to provide practical help with family problems.

Resources for Kids

- Temporary youth shelters where juveniles could live briefly when problems at home reach crisis level would help defuse family tension.
- Youth corps camps during summers. Urban youths need places where there are not just recreational facilities but activities where blacks work with whites and learn how to negotiate, compromise, convey feelings, abide by behavior codes, and so on.
- Schools, parks and recreational programs and centers.

    Schools. Since schools are already in place in neighborhoods, and equipped with gyms, libraries, auditoriums, and plenty of space, some child abuse experts as well as crime fighters are proposing that they be used to a greater extent as community centers. Senator Bill Bradley of New Jersey, for example, submitted a proposal to Congress in 1994 as part of the Clinton administration's crime bill, which called for monies to set up pilot projects in schools that would offer activities and supervision for young people during after-school hours. These areas could also serve as a meeting place for parent support groups and other activities, to help foster a sense of community in areas where it is crumbling.

    Sports programs. In Bensonhurst, Brooklyn, New York, for example, where a white gang gunned down a black teenager for no reason, a basketball program unites kids and youths aged eight to twenty-one, both black and white, in sports. Youths learn to respect each other for who they are, rather than hate each other for their skin color. Other model programs include martial arts training, boxing, football, and other sports.

Arts programs. In the middle of gang territory in Los Angeles, a church group has channeled the activities of one of the most violent gangs in town into a nonviolent, creative form—dancing. Members of the El Salvadoran gang have been taught to perform the nineteenth-century ballet *Sleeping Beauty*. "They used to hang out at street corners because they had this very powerful feeling of us vs. them that they didn't know how to handle," says one coordinator. But since being taken to theaters and sports areas, gang members "have learned acceptable behavior . . . people don't stare them down with hate."[5]

- Wider opportunities for youths. Whether through grants for community projects or government-sponsored jobs, urban youths need projects that require their skills and talents. The National Crime Prevention Council, for example, provides small grants to local community service projects that are run by teens. Tax incentives to businesses could encourage employers to hire impoverished youths.

- Preventing drug and alcohol abuse. Offer treatment for any child or parent. According to the National Institute on Drug Abuse, 6.5 million Americans suffer problems due to drug use, yet only 250,000 receive treatment at any one time.[6] Since drugs figure centrally in many violent crimes, widespread treatment and prevention are musts.

Some federal government programs that work to prevent drug and alcohol abuse include:

Boys and Girls Clubs of America, which reach out to young people and offer them positive alternatives to drugs.

Community-based Anti-Drug Capacity Building

Communities are trying a variety of ways to combat the rising tide of drug-related violence among youths. This policewoman explains the dangers of drugs to students at a Drug Prevention Fair in a school.

Demonstration Programs, which help communities fight drug use.

Congress of National Black Churches Anti-Drug Abuse Program, which involves churches in urban areas to fight drug use and trafficking.

Super Teams, which use peer counseling and professional athletes to combat peer pressure and drug and alcohol abuse.

- Preventing teen pregnancy. Since so many young girls end up mothering children who grow up troubled, some experts believe in trying to curb teen pregnancy by instituting rewards (for example, job training, scholarships) for girls who don't have babies until a certain age. If they do have children, rather than giving them cash in terms of welfare or Aid to Dependent Children, group facilities could provide counseling, job training, and parenting skills.
- Alternative-family support systems. Residences such as the House of Umoja in Philadelphia are run by community leaders. They take in gang members, teaching them to live by a creed of respect, and training them to be members of youth patrols, security guards, elderly escorts, home renovators, day care providers, and lock installers, or to run a youth-operated business.
- Instituting more community-based day programs for juvenile offenders such as:

  New Pride of Colorado, where youths receive daily counseling, job training, education, living skills, and run a business together.

  Schools for suspended students.

  Street Law Diversion Programs, as in Washington, D.C., and at least five other cities, where first-time offenders, aged thirteen to sixteen, meet once a week to argue about their rights and responsibilities, participate in mock trials, act out crimes of violence, and listen to police and judges give presentations.

Clinical Regional Support Teams, as in Florida, where college students act as probation officers for juveniles.

- Providing meaningful jobs for urban and troubled youths that could lead to self-respect and higher-skilled positions. Without a legal means of obtaining support, teens will continue to turn to drugs and illegal, often violent, ways of making money.

SCHOOLS AND EDUCATIONAL PROGRAMS

- Keep kids in school. A Harris poll reported that 90 percent of Americans support special school programs to keep children in school.[7] Quitting school is a strong predictor for trouble ahead—60 percent of prison inmates are high school dropouts. More special programs and alternative schools for teen offenders, the learning disabled, the handicapped, and pregnant teens or young mothers are needed, as well as special counselors for kids at risk for dropping out. This would help curb delinquency, which all too often leads to gangs and youth violence.
- End Truancy. In early 1994, New York City police and the Board of Education launched a joint effort to gather up teenagers who are cutting school and return them to their classes. As part of this plan to curb youth violence, more than 100 police officers work exclusively with this program. Other cities have similar programs, including Philadelphia, Atlanta, St. Louis, San Jose, New Orleans, and Washington, D.C. In Philadelphia, businesses reported a 20 percent drop in juvenile crime after the truancy program began.[8]
- Focus on young black boys. To boost the self-esteem and expectations of young black males, some edutors are stressing that elementary school-age black /s should be separated from girls and taught by ːk male teachers who can give them specialized

attention and be positive role models. Such programs in Florida and Washington have had encouraging results.[9]

- Intervention for problem children and their families. Identifying and aiding children at risk could also help to break the cycle of violence. Counseling, conflict resolution, and parenting-skills classes must be provided to troubled and stressed families.
- Violence prevention programs.

One curriculum in Massachusetts consists of ten lessons for ninth- and tenth-graders, featuring, for example, facts about personal violence and how to cope with anger, how to argue, and how to practice alternatives to fighting.

Also in Massachusetts, some young offenders attend a special Violence Prevention Curriculum for Adolescents for five to ten days, to learn communication skills when anger threatens to tear one apart. Some youths write and/or act in videos about violence, thereby learning how anger and patterns of violence emerge.

Several curricula from the National Crime Prevention Council, such as "Teens, Crime and the Community" and "Making a Difference," help teens learn how to make their schools safer. The programs require all segments of the community to cooperate in making their communities safer, with "block watches" between schools and home, teaching ways to prevent crime, and using teens as peer counselors and patrol persons in parks and public places. Such programs not only help make communities safer but give teens responsibility and a stake in their community.

Kids, said John Calhoun, Executive Director of the National Crime Prevention Council, are too often viewed as

the source of problems, not as a neglected resource and a remarkable source of talent and creativity. Kids are reaching puberty earlier, yet society says, "We don't have a place for you until later." So much goes into bottling the energy rather than using it to help enrich the community. Community crime prevention offers new vistas for permitting and encouraging young people in positive and valued contributions to their friends, families, and communities.[10]

- Career education and mentor programs in junior and senior high schools might help pave the way to a more responsible future for some youths.
- Outward Bound and VisionQuest programs—where youths participate in adventure living, receive personalized therapy, and work themselves up a status ladder—have had low recidivism rates.[11]
- Children of War program brings youths aged thirteen to twenty from other countries to lecture in U.S. schools. The foreign students tell of violence and battles in El Salvador, South Africa, Cambodia, and other countries. Organizers hope that such tales will give courage to American teens fighting drug abuse, gang war, crime, and family violence.

THE CULTURE

Reducing Violence in the Media

As discussed in Chapter Six, consumers must pressure the television, music, and movie industries to stop glorifying violence in front of children. Prime-time television and children's programming need to be more responsible by showing less violence. The Parents Music Resource Center is demanding that warning labels be placed on music albums that have violent or sex-related lyrics. Less sensationalized news coverage of violent crimes, including suicides, would help curb copycat crimes. If the media were to condemn violence, the way it has responded to smoking and drinking while

Among the programs that help young
people gain self-esteem and avoid
destructive patterns is VisionQuest,
where teens participate in outdoor
activities and personalized therapy.

driving, public opinion could shift away from the glorification of violence to the condemnation of violence.

Gun Control

If teens had far less access to lethal weapons, they would obviously not be able to cause as much damage. The Gun Free School Zones Act of 1990 prohibits guns in or near a school, and Congress is considering a federal law that would ban the use of guns among juveniles around the nation (more than 18 states already have such laws). The Brady law, which went into effect in early 1994, now requires that all prospective gun purchasers wait five days, during which time a background check is to be conducted. A follow-up to that law is Brady II, which has been submitted to Congress. Some suggestions include:

- The registration or licensing of all firearms
- The banning of handguns among the public
- Requiring gun and hunting clubs to store and lock up all their members' firearms on club property
- More severe punishment for weapons offenses
- Gun swap programs where people exchange their guns for money or even gift certificates to toy stores. When New York City tried such a program in early 1994, hundreds of guns were exchanged for cash within several days. In 1991, St. Louis collected almost 8,500 firearms, although 1993 still broke the record for the number of gun-related homicides. In Los Angeles, 1,000 guns were surrendered when tickets to big basketball games were offered in their stead.[12]

LAW AND ORDER

- Although it is costly, some cities are putting more detectives on the streets to crack down on illegal gun possession, and are updating computer programs employed to track unregistered guns. New York City, for example, has an estimated 200 million unregistered handguns, which police claim are used in most of the 5,500 shootings every year. The mayor promised in 1994 to almost double the size of the detective staff, to remove as many firearms as possible from the streets.[13]

- An increase in the number of police patrolling streets has also been recommended. According to *U.S. News and World Report,* the country spends some $35 billion a year paying its 535,000 police officers—less money than we spend annually on soft drinks; 3.3 violent crimes per police officer are now committed.[14] President Clinton's 1994 anticrime proposal calls for hiring 50,000 more police officers, and another 50,000 in the future.

- Some experts recommend stricter jail sentences for repeat offenders. The Clinton administration proposed in 1994 a "three strikes and you're out" policy, whereby convicted felons would be given lifetime sentences after three convictions for serious violent crimes.

- Other proposals before Congress in 1994 include: allocating money for more prisons; military-style boot camps instead of prison for first-time offenders; and mandatory sentencing guidelines, including longer prison terms and fewer paroles. Some propose expanding the list of crimes punishable by death, including drive-by shootings, and giving more federal help to local police officials in prosecuting gangs, such as better witness protection plans to encourage gang members to testify against other gang members. Finally, there are proposals to establish better undercover operations, and keep gang members off the streets between the time they are arrested and the time they stand trial.

- Another Clinton suggestion is a "police corps," whereby young people would be trained to serve as police officers in exchange for college tuition.
- Police can flush out criminals from housing projects and then guard the projects so that criminals don't re-enter. Residents and police must, some experts say, "show aggressive contempt, not cringeing respect" for the men and teens who terrorize them and their families.[15]

JUVENILE JUSTICE

Teens know that if they are underage they are virtually immune to punishment. If of legal age, they are still rarely punished for their first or second offenses. When they are to be punished, the criminal justice system is so unwieldy that by the time the youth is sentenced, the crime is long forgotten and disassociated with the punishment. Worse yet, the ones who get caught are those who botched their illegal job—going to jail or a youth facility sends them to the experts. They come out as trained professionals, more angry than when they went in and more eager for revenge.

Studies show that when youngsters get into trouble with the law, they can be deflected from a pattern of crime at an early age. By the time a person commits serious enough crimes to be arrested and convicted, it's often too late to change him.

Some suggestions to improve the juvenile justice system include:

- Doing away with secrecy. Currently, many court records and juvenile histories are secret. Even judges don't have access to previous records. Since early violence is known as the best predictor of later violence, authorities need access to an individual's past record, regardless of how old he or she was or is. Without that knowledge, youths at risk cannot even be identified for special programs and intervention, and the public as well as policy makers cannot make informed decisions.

- Increasing intervention with juvenile delinquents to prevent their becoming offenders. One successful program involves linking each delinquent with a community volunteer, similar to the "Big Brother" and "Big Sister" concept. One such program in Nebraska showed a 62 percent reduction in offenses by youths involved in the program.[16]

- Instituting a consistent pattern of penalties, tailored to age, that are *swiftly* executed for *all* crimes, regardless of age. But offenders should be locked up only as a last resort. Many studies show that delinquents end up more violent and crime-prone after incarceration. Those released end up committing more serious crimes than those treated leniently. Suggestions include mandatory violence prevention classes, community service, fines, and making restitution to the victim.

- Testing routinely for drugs and alcohol in arrested suspects and intervening appropriately with treatment when such substances are found.

- Instituting a system in which punishment is executed swiftly. Fear of punishment is a strong deterrent, but only when it is immediate.

- Using restitution programs for juvenile crime as a substitute for imprisonment or probation. A study of almost 900 teens in six cities showed that juveniles who had to pay back their victims or do community service committed fewer crimes later when compared to teens who were imprisoned and later put on probation.[17]

- Establishing minimum sentences for the most violent crimes. But, rather than locking youths up with adult criminals, placements should be strictly supervised and structured to change behavior as much as possible. These incarcerated youths should also work to help defray their costs in an institution.

• Integrating the juvenile system with its adult counterpart so that there are not two but only one criminal system.

• Since only a small number of juveniles commit most of the violent crime, some experts stress that prosecutors' offices should target chronic offenders for increased resources and more experienced prosecutors. Such cases should not only receive more diagnostic tests, individual treatment plans, and continuous case management but should also be handled swiftly and efficiently while holding the youths more accountable for their actions.

• Instituting a far-reaching program to intervene with chronic violent offenders, for these "are the boys who start early, go on interrupted only by time spent locked up, and wind up in the adult criminal system," [18] says author Rita Kramer.

• Lowering the age at which juveniles who commit a vicious crime may be tried as adults. This recommendation, however, is controversial. Although 75 percent of Americans believe that children who commit violent crimes should be tried as adults,[19] some experts disagree. They maintain that many children make mistakes and, if these children are tried as adults, they will lose important educational opportunities and be scarred for life as "ex-cons." The criminal courts are so overcrowded, they argue, that children might be given lighter sentences here than in juvenile court. Furthermore, trying all children as adults will lower the age of adulthood, and punish children for the failure of society to offer better opportunities and hope to high-risk children.

• Following the course that Massachusetts took—that is, sending only the most dangerous youths to secured treatment centers. Others would go home under supervision or live at special residence centers. Every day, the juveniles would receive counseling, educational and vocational training, and therapy to change their behavioral responses. Between 1978 and 1984, under this type of program, juvenile crime in Massachusetts fell 26 percent, and half the number of juveniles became adult criminals, compared to previous years.[20]

- Community service. One program in Los Angeles puts juvenile offenders who are on probation to work in a facility for handicapped children. The gang members earn high school credit and work experience by helping children with cerebral palsy and other serious disabilities. Some youths come to realize that others are worse off than they are and have even fewer choices, but that they themselves can make a choice and do something useful. Alfred, a Crips youth gang member on probation for being an accomplice in a shooting, says: "This shows that I can do something. It's the first time I've felt like that. I feel more kindhearted and stuff than I thought I was, and I'm not scared to admit it or nothing."[21]

ALTERNATIVES TO PRISON

A list of alternative placements to prison and youth detention facilities is included in Chapter Eight. Specific techniques that have had some success in retraining juvenile delinquents and offenders include:

- Role-playing. Having a group of offenders act as victims and be victimized by assailants teaches offenders what it is like to suffer at the hands of a violent criminal.
- Family therapy. The entire family of a juvenile delinquent or offender is taught together how to negotiate and communicate.

- Withholding rewards and privileges. At Crossroads, a long-term facility in New York City for hard-to-place violent minors, youngsters must earn private rooms and live by a set of norms that require hard work, cooperation, and positive attitudes.
- A model private program in Ohio, called the Paint Creek Youth Center, incorporates many of these techniques and more. The community-based residential center emphasizes personal responsibility toward rules, and peer and staff confrontations about lying, denying blame, intimidation, and lack of empathy for victims. Youths earn points for privileges and promotions while participating in community service projects and work programs. Intensive recreational drug/alcohol treatment, education, and living-skills programs, as well as family therapy, are integral components of the program. Juveniles learn to take responsibility, manage anger and aggressive tendencies, and plan for the future with an arsenal of newly learned skills and improved self-esteem. Although such a program is costly, preliminary results indicate an overwhelming success rate.

PROTECTING YOURSELF

Learning about what society can do to prevent teen violence is one thing; learning how to protect yourself is another. Here are some tips from the National Crime Prevention Council on personal safety:

- Walk with confidence; stay in well-lit areas; at night only walk in groups. Never wear clothes or shoes that won't allow you to run.
- Never leave your keys in the car. Keep the doors locked at all times, both when you are in the car and away from it.
- Learn self-defense and choose a program that teaches you how to be firm and assertive with an

attacker. However, experts advise that sometimes it is better to give up your valuables rather than take a stand.

- If you choose to carry tear gas or pepper spray, be trained properly in their use to ensure they are not taken away and used against you.
- Do whatever you can to stay out of a stranger's car.
- Don't blame yourself if you do become a victim. You may choose to seek counseling; being a victim can be a very upsetting and traumatic experience.

CONCLUSION

Violence is like a disease that is slowly sapping the vitality and lifeblood of our society. It affects us all. Social injustice, poverty and the frustration it breeds, bigotry, and fear all feed the disease. The police and the courts alone can't fix the problem, for at the heart of the teen violence epidemic is a severe breakdown of the values of community, family and work. Youths bear the brunt of the pain of poverty, hopelessness, and violence caused by the deterioration of society. If not challenged head-on, violence will continue to spread and infect more individuals, families, schools, communities, and cities.

As teens wade through the turbulent waters of adolescence, they are constantly trying to cope with the emotional intensity and behavioral swings that are so common during this period. They yearn for a sense of mastery and control over their lives and environment. At the same time, they are enormously susceptible to influences and pressures around them. Almost all teens, whether impoverished or privileged, are impatient, impressionable, and vulnerable, and they learn by imitating those around them.

When their environment, however, is one riddled with poverty and neglect, where guns lie casually around, where unemployment, alcohol and drug abuse are rampant, and where violence is commonplace, the teenagers will inevitably adapt to that kind of life and adopt its savage ways. As a result, too many teens are learning that violence is the way to settle disputes. They are becoming less and less apt to express anger with words or fists, but rather to pull out a gun.

Caught in a twilight zone of no control, where their world seems to work against them, many youths lack lawful opportunities that challenge their spirit and harness their energy. When offered the rush of a drug high or the thrill of a crime, the temptation for relief from an eternally dreary present can be overwhelming. When the future seems no future at all, the immediate gratification of the present becomes the only thing that matters, regardless of who gets in the way.

Once part of the drug and street-crime culture, many teens fall through the cracks into a pit of powerlessness and hopelessness with no way out. When life loses hope, there's little left to lose. School seems meaningless and many drop out. Too many teens end up illiterate, unemployed, and, to a great extent, unemployable. Impaired by the ravages of drugs and/or alcohol abuse, the ability to make responsible decisions slowly slips away.

If left unchecked, today's troubled teens will perpetuate a legacy of violence for yet another generation, passing it down to the next generation. Increasingly, violence will become a way of life.

All the ingredients for ultimate tragedy are rapidly colliding. The quality of our lives is slowly being eroded, threatened by the violent society and the violent children it is fostering. We must act to do our part, to nourish the emotional, intellectual, and behavioral development of all children. We must provide meaningful alternatives to the seductive lure of street crime, drugs, and violence, and we must institute stern, swift,

Most teenagers want to be useful, contributing members of society. These high school students in Tucson, Arizona, declare their own war on drugs through the use of dance, music, and song in programs they put on for other students.

and consistent penalties for those who commit violent acts.

Slowing the cycle of violence will be painstaking and expensive, requiring dramatic changes in the socioeconomic and cultural fabric of our society, and visionary and extraordinary commitments on the federal, state, and local levels.

If those in power continue to allow a permanent underclass to exist, imprisoned in inner-city ghettos or quietly forgotten in rural areas, the disease of violence will fester and finally abscess, spewing its infection at random.

Teenagers desperately want to play a vital and active role in contributing to family and community. Representative George Miller of California, as chairman of the House Select Committee on Children, Youth, and Families, has heard testimony from experts on how to curb teen violence. He says:

> *By failing to provide young people . . . with legitimate outlets for their talents, we are squandering the energy and resourcefulness of their youth. By doing so, we not only deny them the chance to participate in the American dream, we assure that our own dreams will be diminished by the cost of their failure.*[22]

If we neglect to devote our fullest abilities and resources to battle violence, and teen violence in particular, in today's society, the disease will inexorably spread until it rots the very soul of our society. We can't afford to wait.

APPENDIX
WHERE TO GET MORE INFORMATION

Building Bridges
Harvard Negotiation Project
Harvard Law School
Pound Hall, Room 513
Cambridge, MA 02138
617-495-1684
(Offers a peer-taught curriculum for high schools on how to handle conflict.)

Center to Prevent Handgun Violence
1225 Eye Street NW, Suite 1100
Washington, D.C. 20005
202-289-7319
(This nonprofit organization to prevent gun violence has a pre-K through 12th grade curriculum called STAR. It also offers educational programs and teacher training on handgun violence prevention.)

Cities in Schools
1023 15th Street NW, Suite 600
Washington, D.C. 20005

Committee for Children
Seattle, WA
800-634-4449
(This nonprofit organization has the Second Step program, a K through 8th grade curriculum that teaches children empathy, how to control anger, reduce aggressiveness, and generally boost social competence.)

Educators for Social Responsibility, Conflict Resolution Program
23 Garden Street
Cambridge, MA 02138
617-492-1764
(Program for all grade levels, which addresses conflict resolution, violence prevention, prejudice reduction, communication skills, emotional expression, and multicultural awareness.)

Elementary School Conflict Managers Program
School Initiatives Program
Community Board Center for Policy and Training
149 9th Street
San Francisco, CA 94103
(Offers a five-day curriculum in conflict management and communication skills.)

Institute for Mental Health Initiatives
Channeling Children's Anger
4545 42nd Street NW, Suite 311
Washington, D.C. 20016
202-364-7111
(Offers materials on teaching anger-management skills to teens and their parents.)

National Association for Mediation in Education
425 Amity Street
Amherst, MA 01002
413-545-2462
(Offers materials for training kids, teachers, and parents in conflict resolution.)

National Center for Juvenile Justice
701 Forbes Avenue
Pittsburgh, PA 15219
412-227-6950

National Crime Prevention Council
733 15th Street NW, Suite 540
Washington, D.C. 20005
202-466-6272
(Offers a curriculum to help teens protect themselves by focusing on such areas as child and drug abuse, teen pregnancy, and literacy.)

National Coalition on Television Violence
P.O. Box 2157
Champaign, IL 61820
217-384-1920

National Institute for Violence Prevention
P.O. Box 1035
Sandwich, MA 02563
508-833-0731
(Offers training in violence-prevention strategies and program development.)

National School Safety Center (NSSC)
16830 Ventura Boulevard, Suite 200
Encino, CA 91436
818-377-6200
(Provides training and help with school crime prevention. Publisher of handbook *Gangs in Schools;* also publishes information on gangs, weapons, crisis management, and planning for safer schools.)

Office of Juvenile Justice and Delinquency Prevention
Juvenile Justice Clearing House
Box 600
Rockville, MD 20850
or 633 Indiana Avenue NW, Washington, D.C. 20531
800-638-8736

Resolving Conflict Creatively
163 Third Avenue, Suite 230
New York, NY 10003
212-260-6290
(Offers conflict resolution and peer mediation programs.)

Super Teams
1411 K Street NW, Suite 910
Washington, D.C. 20005
202-783-1533

Tough Love
P.O. Box 1069
Doylestown, PA 18901
800-333-1069

National Crime Hot Lines
School Crime Stoppers
800-245-0009

WeTip
800-782-7463
(They offer tips to prevent violence and seek reports on school violence.)

SOURCE NOTES

Chapter One: True Stories
1. "The Youth Crime Plague," *Time,* July 11, 1977, p. 18.
2. Stephen Sawicki, "The Violent Young," *Cleveland,* July 1986, p. 79.
3. Ibid.
4. Ibid.
5. Peter Wilkinson, "Darkness at the Heart of Town,'' *Rolling Stone,* October 5, 1989, p. 55.
6. Ibid.
7. Ibid.
8. David E. Pitt, "Gang Attack: Unusual for Its Viciousness," *New York Times,* April 25, 1989, p. B1.
9. George F. Will, "Calling 'Wilding' Exactly What It Is: Evil," *Los Angeles Times,* May 1, 1989.
10. Michael Stone, "What Really Happened in Central Park," *New York,* August 14, 1989, p. 41.
11. Michael Kaufman, "Park Suspects: Children of Discipline," *New York Times,* April 26, 1989, p. A1.
12. Stone, p. 33.
13. Ibid., p. 41.

Chapter Two: Our Violent Society
1. Robert Baker and Sandra Ball, *Mass Media and Violence,* vol. 9, *A Report to the National Commission on the Causes and Prevention of Violence* (Washington, D.C.: U.S. Government Printing Office, 1969), p. 55; and John Gunn, *Violence* (New York: Praeger Publishers, 1973), p. 83.
2. Gilda Berger, *Violence and Drugs* (New York: Franklin Watts, 1989), pp. 12–13.
3. John Gunn, *Violence* (New York: Praeger, 1993), pp. 82–83.
4. Lynn A. Curtis, "Race and Violent Crime," in Neil Alan Weiner and Marvin E. Wolfgang, eds., *Violent Crime, Violent Criminals* (Newbury Park, Calif.: Sage Publications, 1989), p. 140.
5. Don B. Kates, Jr., "Why Gun Laws Won't Stop Shootings," *New York Times,* February 4, 1989, p. 27.
6. Ted Gest, "Violence in America," *U.S. News & World Report,* January 17, 1994, p. 24, quoting statistics from the FBI.
7. Ibid., p. 27.
8. Judy Keen, " 'One Cannot Feel Safe Anyplace,' " *USA Today,* January 25, 1994, p. 1.
9. Ibid., p. 27.

10. Marty Baumann, "Besieged by Crime," *USA Today,* January 25, 1994, p. 1, quoting FBI crime reports.
11. Andrew H. Malcolm, "More Americans Are Killing Each Other," *New York Times,* December 31, 1989.
12. "FBI Report Confirms Sharp Rise in Violent Crime," *New York Times,* August 6, 1990.
13. Ibid.
14. Robert S. Clarke, Ph.D., *Deadly Force, The Lure of Violence* (Springfield, Ill.: Charles C. Thomas, 1988), p. 8.
15. Gest, p. 26
16. Evan Stark, "The Myth of Black Violence," *New York Times,* July 18, 1990, p. A6
17. Curtis, p. 140.
18. Marvin E. Wolfgang et al., *From Boy to Man, from Delinquency to Crime* (University of Chicago Press, 1987), pp. 118–20.
19. Stark.
20. Nancy R. Needham, "Kids Who Kill," *NEA Today,* February 1988, p. 10.
21. Wolfgang, p. 118.

Chapter Three: A Violent Society Breeds Violent Children
 1. Stephen Sawicki, "The Violent Young," *Cleveland,* July 1986, p. 81.
 2. Steven J. Apter and Arnold P. Goldstein, *Youth Violence: Programs and Prospects* (New York: Pergamon Press, 1986), p. 140.
 3. David Relin, "The Juvenile Justice System: Portrait of a Crisis," *Scholastic Update,* November 4, 1988, p. 6.
 4. Apter and Goldstein, p. 140.
 5. Ronald S. Lauder, *Fighting Violent Crime in America* (New York: Dodd, Mead, 1985), p. 25.
 6. Barbara Allen-Hagen and Melissa Sickmund, Ph.D., "Juveniles and Violence: Juvenile Offending and Victimization," *Office of Juvenile Justice and Delinquency Prevention Fact Sheet,* July 1993.
 7. Andrew H. Malcolm, "New Strategies to Fight Crime Go Far Beyond Stiffer Terms and More Cells," *New York Times,* October 10, 1990.
 8. Anastasia Toufexis, "Our Violent Kids," *Time,* June 12, 1989, p. 52.
 9. Charles Patrick Ewing, *Kids Who Kill* (New York: Lexington Books, 1990).
10. "Teenagers and Crime," *Good Housekeeping,* November 1989, p. 270.
11. Howard N. Snyder, Ph.D. "Arrests of Youth 1990," *Office of Juvenile Justice and Delinquency Prevention Update on Statistics,* U.S. Department of Justice, January 1992.
12. Ibid., p. 270.
13. Snyder, p. 270.
14. Connie Leslie, "Girls Will be Girls," *Newsweek,* August 2, 1993, p. 44.
15. Toufexis.
16. Marvin E. Wolfgang et al., *From Boy to Man, from Delinquency to Crime* (University of Chicago Press, 1987), pp. 118–20.
17. Evan Stark, "The Myth of Black Violence," *New York Times,* August 18, 1990.

18. Isabel Wilkerson, "Facing Grim Data on Young Males, Blacks Grope for Ways to End Blight," *New York Times,* July 17, 1990.

19. Clemens Bartollas, *Juvenile Delinquency* (New York: John Wiley, 1985), p. 365.

20. Ibid., p. 366.

21. Neil Alan Weiner and Marvin E. Wolfgang, *Violent Crime, Violent Criminals* (Newbury Park, Calif.: Sage Publications, 1989), p. 102.

22. Hakan Stattin and David Magnusson, "The Role of Early Aggressive Behavior in the Frequency, Seriousness, and Types of Later Crime," *Journal of Consulting and Clinical Psychology,* 1989, vol. 57, no. 6, pp. 710–18.

23. Lauder, pp. 25–26.

24. Jeff Coplon, "Young, Bad & Dangerous," *Ladies' Home Journal,* August 1985, p. 165.

25. Ibid.

26. Lauder, pp. 67–69.

27. Peter Applebome, "Juvenile Crime: the Offenders Are Younger and the Offenses More Serious," *New York Times,* February 3, 1987, p. 8.

28. Barbara Kantrowitz, "Wild in the Streets," *Newsweek,* August 2, 1993, p. 42.

29. Ted Gest, p. 27.

30. Lauder, p. 52.

31. Applebome.

32. Lauder, p. 55.

33. Ibid.

34. Ibid., p. 58.

35. David Relin, "The Juvenile Justice System: Portrait of a Crisis," *Scholastic Update,* November 4, 1988, p. 7.

36. "The Typical Teen Offender," *Scholastic Update,* November 4, 1988, p. 3.; and Josh Getlin, "39% of Incarcerated Juveniles Found Jailed for Violence," *Los Angeles Times,* September 19, 1988, p. 2.

37. "Targeting the Children," *Time,* November 6, 1989, p. 36.

38. Barbara Allen-Hagen and Melissa Sickmund, p. 2.

39. Barbara Kantrowitz, "Wild in the Streets, *Newsweek,* August 2, 1993, p. 43.

40. Ibid., p. 43.

41. Ibid., p. 43.

42. Robert Davis, "For Kids, Life On A Hair Trigger," *USA Today,* February 3, 1994, p. 3A.

43. Ibid.

44. Jerry Adler, "Kids Growing Up Scared," *Newsweek,* January 10, 1994, p. 44., citing FBI Uniform Crime Reports.

45. Anita Manning, "Gunshot kills One U.S. Child Every Two Hours," *USA Today,* January 21, 1994, p. 1.

46. Deborah Prothrow-Smith, M.D., with Michael Weissman, "Deadly Consequences: How Violence is Destroying Our Teenage Population and A Plan To Begin Solving the Problem" (New York: HarperCollins), 1991, p. 3.

47. Barbara Allen-Hagen and Melissa Sickmund, Ph.D., "Juveniles and Vio-

lence: Juvenile Offending and Victimization," Office of Juvenile Justice and Delinquency Prevention, Fact Sheet, July 1993.

48. Michael R. Greenberg, George W. Carey, and Frank J. Popper, "Violent Death, Violent States, and American Youth," *Public Interest,* spring 1987, p. 38.

49. Barbara Allen-Hagen, p. 4.

50. Nancy R. Needham, "Kids Who Kill," *NEA Today,* February 1988, p. 10.

51. John A. Calhoun, "Violence, Youth and a Way Out," *Children Today,* September–October, p. 9.

52. Wolfgang, *From Boy to Man,* pp. 200–01.

Chapter Four: The Psychology of Violence and Adolescence

1. Jeff Coplon, "Young, Bad & Dangerous," *Ladies' Home Journal,* August 1985, p. 166.

2. Rollo May, *Power and Innocence: A Search for the Sources of Violence* (New York: Norton, 1972), pp. 182, 243, 245.

3. John Gunn, *Violence* (New York: Praeger, 1973), p. 57.

4. May, pp. 23, 37.

5. Ibid., p. 182.

6. Ibid., pp. 182, 187–188.

7. Daniel Goleman, "Taming Unruly Boys: Old Techniques and New Approaches," *New York Times,* February 1, 1990, p. B10.

8. Jonathan H. Pincus, "A Neurological View of Violence," in David H. Crowell, *Childhood Aggression and Violence: Sources of Influence, Prevention, and Control* (New York: Plenum Press, 1987), pp. 53–73.

9. Anastasia Toufexis, "Our Violent Kids," *Time,* June 12, 1989, p. 52.

10. "The Origins of Youthful Violence," *Harvard Medical School Mental Health Letter,* January 1990, vol. 6, no. 7, p. 7.

11. Ronald Kotulak, "Why Some Kids Turn Out Bad," *Chicago Tribune,* December 27, 1993, p. A1.

12. Ibid. p. A8.

13. Anastasia Toufexis, "Seeking the Roots of Violence," *Time,* April 19, 1993, p. 53.

14. Beatrix Hamburg, "Themes and Variations of Adolescence," in Action for Children's Television, *TV & Teens: Experts Look at the Issues* (Reading, Mass.: Addison-Wesley, 1982), p. 8.

15. Judith Viorst, *Necessary Losses* (New York: Fawcett Gold Medal, 1986), p. 160.

16. Felton Earls, "The Social Reconstruction of Adolescence: Toward an Explanation for Increasing Rates of Violence in Youth," *Perspectives in Biology and Medicine,* autumn 1978, p. 65.

17. David Bakan, "Adolescence in America: From Idea to Social Fact," *Daedalus,* Fall 1971, in Dean G. Rojek and Gary F. Jensen, *Readings in Juvenile Delinquency* (Lexington, Mass.: D.C. Heath, 1982), p. 32.

18. Earls, p. 72.

19. Marc Fisher, "The Word on the Street is Death," *Washington Post,* February 12, 1989, p. C1.

20. John A. Calhoun, "Violence, Youth and a Way Out," *Children Today,* September–October, p. 9.

21. Cheryl Carpenter et al., *Kids, Drugs, and Crime* (Lexington, Mass.: Lexington Books, 1988), p. 99.
22. Jeff Coplon, "Young, Bad and Dangerous," *Ladies' Home Journal*, August 1985, p. 166.
23. Barbara Kantravitz, Wild in the Streets," *Newsweek*, August 2, 1993, p. 43.
24. Clemens Bartollas, *Juvenile Delinquency* (New York: John Wiley, 1985), p. 160.

Chapter Five: The Legacy of Family Violence
1. *Time*, December 21, 1987, in Gilda Berger, *Violence and the Family* (New York: Franklin Watts, 1990), p. 9.
2. Larry Hebert, M.D., "Life Cycle of Violence," in Annette Zimmern Reed, Ph.D., *Violence in America* (Austin, Tex.: Family Advocacy Program, U.S. Air Force, 1987), p. 13.
3. Ibid., p. 17.
4. Suzanne K. Steinmetz and Murray A. Straus, "The Family As Cradle of Violence," *Society*, vol. 10, no. 6, September/October 1973, in Dean G. Rojek and Gary F. Jensen, *Readings in Juvenile Delinquency* (Lexington, Mass.: D.C. Heath, 1982), p. 233.
5. Daniel Goleman, "Hope Seen for Curbing Youth Violence," *New York Times*, August 11, 1993, p. A10.
6. Gilda Berger, *Violence and the Family* (New York: Franklin Watts, 1990), p. 57.
7. Ibid., p. 59.
8. "The Origins of Youthful Violence," *Harvard Medical School Mental Health Letter*, January 1990, vol. 6, no. 7, p. 7.
9. University of Washington, "When Violence Begets Violence," *Science Digest*, January 1990, p. 97.
10. Clemens Bartollas, *Juvenile Delinquency* (New York: John Wiley, 1985), p. 247.
11. John Gunn, *Violence* (New York: Praeger, 1973), p. 65.
12. Dr. Jerome Miller, as interviewed on "Teens Who've Committed Violent Crimes," "The Oprah Winfrey Show," TV broadcast on ABC, June 23, 1989.
13. Meda Chesney-Lind, "Girls and Violence," in David H. Crowell, et al., eds., *Childhood Aggression and Violence: Sources of Influence, Prevention, and Control* (New York: Plenum Press, 1987), pp. 207–29.
14. Ibid.
15. Rita Kramer, *At a Tender Age: Violent Youth and Juvenile Justice* (New York: Holt & Co., 1988), p. 213.
16. Ibid., p. 215.
17. Ibid., p. 220.
18. Jerry Adler, "Kids Growing Up Scared," *Newsweek*, January 10, 1994, p. 44.
19. Kramer, p. 212.
20. "Wilding."
21. "Peter Uhlenberg and David Eggebeen, "The Declining Well-Being of American Adolescents," *The Public Interest*, Winter 1986, p. 37.

22. Anastasia Toufexis, "Our Violent Kids," *Time,* June 12, 1989, p. 52.

23. Jill Smolowe, "Danger in the Safety Zone," *Time,* August 23, 1993, p. 32.

24. Ibid., p. 38.

25. Stephen Sawicki, "The Violent Young," *Cleveland,* July 1986, p. 148.

26. Anastasia Toufexis, "Our Violent Kids," *Time,* June 12, 1989, p. 52.

Chapter Six: The Impact of Community and Culture on Teen Violence

1. Anastasia Toufexis, "Our Violent Kids," *Time,* June 12, 1989, p. 52.

2. John A. Calhoun, "Violence, Youth, and a Way Out," *Children Today,* September–October 1988, p. 10.

3. Alex Kutlowitz, "Day-to-Day Violence Takes a Terrible Toll on Inner-City Youth," *Wall Street Journal,* October 27, 1987, p. 1.

4. Bob Herbert, "Deadly Data on Handguns," *New York Times,* March 2, 1994.

5. Kutlowitz, p. 1.

6. "U.S. Panel Warns on Child Poverty," *New York Times,* April 29, 1990.

7. William Pfaff, " 'Wilding' in New York, Moral Void in America," *Los Angeles Times,* May 7, 1989.

8. Bill Moyers, *A World of Ideas* (New York: Doubleday, 1988), p. 6.

9. Kutlowitz, p. 45.

10. Gilda Berger, *Violence and the Media* (New York: Franklin Watts, 1989), p. 18.

11. Dave Rhein, "The Staggering Statistics on Television Violence Deserve Consideration," Gannett News Service, *Ithaca Journal,* January 29, 1988, p. 16TV.

12. "Lawmakers Urge Action to Reduce Violence on Television Shows," Associated Press, *Ithaca Journal,* January 26, 1990, p. 7A.

13. Susan Chira, "Hillary Clinton Seeks Balance in News Coverage of Violence," *New York Times,* March 4, 1994, p. 7.

14. Jeffrey H. Goldstein, *Aggression and Crimes of Violence* (New York: Oxford University Press, 1986), p. 40.

15. Daniel Goleman, "Hope Seen for Curbing Youth Violence," *New York Times,* August 11, 1993, p. A10.

16. Toufexis, p. 52.

17. Jerry Adler, "Kids Growing Up Scared," *Newsweek,* January 10, 1994, p. 44.

18. Elizabeth Brown, M.D., and William R. Hendee, Ph.D., "Adolescents and Their Music," *Journal of the American Medical Association,* September 22/29, 1989, vol. 262, no. 12, pp. 1659–63.

19. Hilary Appelman, Associated Press, "Random Brutal Crimes on Rise," *Ithaca Journal,* February 10, 1990.

20. Warren E. Leary, "Gloomy Report on the Health of Teen-Agers," *New York Times,* June 9, 1990, p. 3.

Chapter Seven: Guns and Drugs

1. Ted Gest, "Violence in America," *U.S. News & World Report,* January 17, 1994, p. 24.

2. Jeffrey H. Goldstein, *Aggression and Crimes of Violence* (New York:

Oxford University Press, 1986), p. 91.

3. Sarah Brady," . . . And the Case Against Them," *Time,* January 29, 1990, p. 23.
4. Bob Herbert, "Deadly Data on Handguns," *New York Times,* March 2, 1994.
5. "Seven Deadly Days," *Time,* July 17, 1989, p. 31.
6. Andrew H. Malcolm, "More Americans Are Killing Each Other," *New York Times,* December 31, 1989, p. 20.
7. John D. Hull, "A Boy and His Gun," *Time,* August 2, 1993, p. 22.
8. Hull, p. 22.
9. Bob Herbert, "Deadly Data on Handguns," *New York Times,* March 2, 1994.
10. "Handgun Violence: An American Epidemic" (Washington, D.C.: Center to Prevent Handgun Violence), 1989.
11. "Targeting the Children," *Time,* November 6, 1989, p. 36.
12. Hull, p. 22.
13. Herbert, Ibid.
14. Barbara Allen-Hagen and Melissa Sickmund, Ph.D., "Juveniles and Violence: Juvenile Offending and Victimization," Office of Juvenile Justice and Delinquency Prevention, Fact Sheet, July 1993.
15. George Hackett, "Kids: Deadly Force," *Newsweek,* January 11, 1988, p. 18.
16. Hull, p. 22.
17. Ibid.
18. Patrice Gaines-Carter and Lynne Duke, "Guns Mean Status to Some D.C. Youths," *Washington Post,* January 1, 1988, p. 4A.
19. Richard Hofstadter, *American Violence: A Documentary History* in Jack Zevin, *Violence in America: What Is the Alternative?* (Englewood Cliffs, N.J.: Prentice-Hall, 1973), p. 77.
20. Herbert, Ibid.
21. "Kids Who Kill," *Time,* December 2, 1985, p. 66.
22. Hull, p. 23.
23. Andrew H. Malcolm, "More Americans Are Killing Each Other," *New York Times,* December 31, 1989, p. 20.
24. Peter Kerr, "Crime Study Finds Drug Use in Most Arrested," *New York Times,* January 22, 1988, pp. A1, B4, in Gilda Berger, *Violence and Drugs* (New York: Franklin Watts, 1989), p. 10.
25. Leah Eskin, "Punishment or Reform: The History of Juvenile Justice," *Scholastic Update,* November 4, 1988, p. 11.
26. Berger, *Violence and Drugs,* p. 16.
27. Ibid., p. 35.
28. "Kid Killers," *Time,* December 22, 1986.
29. Berger, *Violence and Drugs,* p. 26.
30. Peter Applebome, "Juvenile Crime: The Offenders Are Younger and the Offenses More Serious," *New York Times,* February 3, 1987, p. 8.
31. Seth Mydans, "On Guard Against Gangs at a Los Angeles School," *New York Times,* November 19, 1989, p. 1.
32. Gina Kolata, "Grim Seeds of Park Rampage Found in East Harlem Streets," *New York Times,* May 2, 1989, p. C1.

33. *Violence and Youth: Psychology's Response* (Washington, D.C.: Am. Psych. Assn., 1993), p. 28.

Chapter Eight: Juvenile Justice or Juvenile Joke?

1. Mortimer B. Zuckerman, "Meltdown in Our Cities," *U.S. News & World Report,* May 19, 1989, p. 74.
2. Ibid.
3. "The Youth Crime Plague," *Time,* July 11, 1977, in Dean G. Rojek and Gary F. Jensen, *Readings in Juvenile Delinquency* (Lexington, Mass.: D.C. Heath, 1982), p. 5.
4. Alex Kotlowitz, "Their Crimes Don't Make Them Adults," *New York Times Magazine,* February 13, 1994, p. 40.
5. Ronald S. Lauder, *Fighting Violent Crime in America* (New York: Dodd, Mead, 1985), p. 82.
6. Thomas Toch, "Violence in Schools," *U.S. News & World Report,* November 8, 1993, p. 40.
7. Zuckerman, "War On Crime, By the Numbers," *U.S. News & World Report,* January 17, 1993.
8. Stephen Labaton, "Glutted Probation System Puts Communities in Peril," *New York Times,* June 19, 1990, p. A41.
9. Leonard Buder, "New York to Add Lawyers for Surge in Youth Crimes," *New York Times,* February 28, 1990, p. B3.
10. "More Kids Are Behind Bars," *Scholastic Update,* November 4, 1988, p. 7.
11. Ibid.
12. Curtis Sitomer, "Some Young US Offenders Go to 'Boot Camp'—Others Are Put in Adult Jails," *Christian Science Monitor,* October 27, 1989, p. 31.
13. Steve Manning, "Getting Tough: Does It Work?," *Scholastic Update,* November 4, 1988, p. 8.
14. Lauder, p. 82.
15. Zuckerman, p. 74.
16. Rita Kramer, *At a Tender Age: Violent Youth and Juvenile Justice* (New York: Holt & Co., 1988), p. 226.
17. "The Youth Crime Plague," *Time,* July 11, 1977, in Dean G. Rojek and Gary F. Jensen, *Readings in Juvenile Delinquency* (Lexington, Mass.: D.C. Heath, 1982), p. 8.
18. Kramer, pp. 259–60.

Chapter Nine: Teen Crime Against the Family

1. Gerald C. Lubenow, "When Kids Kill Their Parents," *Newsweek,* June 27, 1983, p. 35.
2. Peter C. Kratcoski and Lucille Dunn Kratcoski, "Turning the Tables: Adolescents' Violent Behavior Toward Their Parents," *USA Today* (the magazine), January 1982, p. 21.
3. Cathy Spatz Widom, "The Intergenerational Transmission of Violence," in Neil A. Weiner and Marvin E. Wolfgang, eds., *Pathways to Criminal Violence* (Newbury Park, Calif.: Sage Publications, 1989), p. 137.
4. Anastasia Toufexis, "When Kids Kill Abusive Parents," *Time,* November 23, 1992, p. 60.

5. Kratcoski.
6. "The Dangerous Years," *Bodywatch,* TV broadcast on PBS on March 11, 1989.
7. Clemens Bartollas, *Juvenile Delinquency* (New York: John Wiley, 1985), p. 365.
8. Jon D. Hull, "Brutal Treatment, Vicious Deed," *Time,* October 19, 1987, p. 68.
9. Ibid.
10. Shelly Post, "Adolescent Parricide in Abusive Families," *Child Welfare,* September–October 1982, pp. 445–55.

Chapter Ten: School Violence
1. George Hackett, "Kids: Deadly Force," *Newsweek,* January 11, 1988, p. 19.
2. Thomas Toch, "Violence in Schools," *U.S. News & World Report,* November 8, 1993, p. 31.
3. Leslie Ansley, "Safety in Schools: 'It Just Keeps Getting Worse,' " *USA Weekend,* August 13–15, 1993, p. 5.
4. Barbara Allen-Hagen and Melissa Sickmund, Ph.D., "Juveniles and Violence: Juvenile Offending and Victimization," Office of Juvenile Justice and Delinquency Prevention, Fact Sheet, July 1993, p. 2.
5. Toch, p. 32.
6. Barbara Kantrowitz, "Wild in the Streets," *Newsweek,* August 2, 1993, p. 43.
7. Ansley, p. 4., citing Lou Harris survey of July 1993.
8. Ibid.
9. Toch, p. 32.
10. Ronald S. Lauder, *Fighting Violent Crime in America* (New York: Dodd, Mead, 1985), p. 73.
11. Ibid. p. 73.
12. Sarah Lyall, "A Losing Fight on Violence in the Schools," *New York Times,* February 17, 1989, p. B1.
13. Dorothy Gilliam, "No Excuse for Neglect," *Washington Post,* January 30, 1989, p. D3.
14. "Chilling the Fashion Rage," *Time,* January 22, 1990, p. 19.
15. Jane Perlez, "Knives and Guns in the Book Bags Strike Fear in a West Side School," *New York Times,* December 10, 1987, p. B1.
16. Lyall.
17. Hackett, p. 19.
18. Digilio.
19. Felicia R. Lee, "When Violence and Terror Strike Outside the Schools," *New York Times,* November 14, 1989, p. B1.
20. Lee, "When Violence and Terror Strike Outside the Schools."
21. Seth Mydans, "On Guard Against Gangs at a Los Angeles School," *New York Times,* November 19, 1989, p. 1.
22. Andrea Fort and Rich Connell, "Transfers Demanded for Students at Jordan High," *Los Angeles Times,* February 18, 1989, p. 1.
23. Needham, p. 11.
24. Lyall.

25. Gest.
26. Needham, p. 18.
27. Mydans.
28. William E. Schmidt, "ACLU Revises Its Strategy in Attempt to Mold Opinion," *New York Times,* January 14, 1990, p. 1.

Chapter Eleven: "Wilding" and Mob Violence
1. "Wilding," *Nightline,* TV broadcast on ABC, May 16, 1989.
2. Ronald Sullivan, "7 Girls Found Guilty in Attacks with Pins on 45 West Side Women," *New York Times,* April 4, 1990, p. A9.
3. Susan Baker and Tipper Gore, "Some Reasons for 'Wilding,' " *Newsweek,* May 29, 1989, p. 6.
4. "Wilding," *The Economist,* April 29, 1989, p. 27.
5. Chapin Wright, "Robbery by Youths on Rise in City," *Newsday,* January 31, 1990, p. 5.
6. Anastasia Toufexis, "Our Violent Kids," *Time,* June 12, 1989, p. 52.
7. Felicia R. Lee, "When Violence and Terror Strike Outside the Schools," *New York Times,* November 14, 1989, p. B1.
8. Wright.
9. Tom Wicker, "The Worst Fear," *New York Times,* April 28, 1989, p. A39.
10. Allan Fotheringham, "The 'Wilding' of the Vanities," *MacLean's,* May 8, 1989, p. 64.
11. Robin Marantz Henig, "The 'Wilding' of Central Park," *Washington Post,* May 2, 1989, p. 6.
12. Ibid.
13. Nancy Gibbs, "Wilding in the Night," *Time,* May 8, 1989, p. 20.
14. Paula Span and Howard Kurtz, "Aftermath of an Assault," *Washington Post,* April 27, 1989, p. A34.
15. David Pitt, "Gang Attack: Unusual for its Viciousness," *New York Times,* April 25, 1989, p. B1.
16. Henig.
17. Michael Stone, "What Really Happened in Central Park," *New York,* August 14, 1989, p. 43.
18. Ibid.
19. Ibid.
20. John Gunn, *Violence* (New York: Praeger Publications, 1973), p. 93.
21. George Will, "Calling 'Wilding' Exactly What It Is: Evil," *Washington Post,* April 30, 1989, p. C7.

Chapter Twelve: Gangs
1. Matt Lait, "The Battle to Control 50,000 Gang Members on the Streets of Los Angeles," *Washington Post,* March 12, 1988, p. A3.
2. Lori Vrcan (sic), "The Growing Threat of Gang Violence," *Schools and College,* May 1988, p. 23.
3. Ibid.
4. Connie Leslie, "Girls Will be Girls," *Newsweek,* August 2, 1993, p. 44.
5. Ibid.; Donald Baker, "The Cancer of Cripping Is Spreading, A Fact We Must Face to Snuff It Out," *Los Angeles Times,* October 16, 1988, p. 5;

and Malcolm W. Klein and Cheryl L. Maxson, "Street Gang Violence," in Neil Alan Weiner and Marvin E. Wolfgang, *Violent Crime, Violent Criminals* (Newbury Park, Calif.: Sage Publications, 1989), p. 200.

6. William B. Sanders, "Juvenile Delinquency: Causes, Patterns, and Reactions" (New York: Holt, Rinehart and Winston), 1981, p. 210.

7. Anastasia Toufexis, "Our Violent Kids," *Time*, June 12, 1989, p. 52.

8. Barbara Kantrowitz, "Wild in the Streets," *Newsweek*, Aug. 2, 1993, p. 44.

9. Ronald S. Lauder, *Fighting Violent Crime in America* (New York: Dodd, Mead, 1985), p. 74.

10. Lait.

11. Scott Armstrong, "Los Angeles Confronts More Youth Violence," *Christian Science Monitor*, February 24, 1988, p. 3.

12. Yumi Wilson, Associated Press, "Teens Who Can't Get Away From Gangs," June 17, 1992.

13. Gilda Berger, *Violence and Drugs* (New York: Franklin Watts, 1989), p. 51.

14. Seth Mydans, "On Guard Against Gangs at a Los Angeles School," *New York Times*, November 19, 1989, p. 1.

15. Office of Juvenile Justice and Delinquency Prevention, *Federal Juvenile Delinquency Programs 1988* (Washington, D.C.: U.S. Department of Justice, 1989), p. 69.

16. Vrcan.

17. Lait.

18. Alex Kotlowitz, "Lords of the Slums: Chicago Street Gangs Treat Public Housing as Private Fortresses," *Wall Street Journal*, September 30, 1988, p. 1.

19. Ibid.

20. Susan Lang. *Extremist Groups in America* (New York: Franklin Watts, 1990), p. 91.

21. Morris Dees, "Young, Gullible and Taught to Hate," *New York Times*, August 25, 1993, p. A15.

22. Jason deParle, "1989 Surge in Anti-Semitic Acts Is Reported by B'nai B'rith," *New York Times*, January 20, 1990, p. C10.

23. Lang, p. 91.

24. Jack Katz and Daniel Marks, "Much of What We Do to Fight Gangs Turns Out to Be Their Best Recruiter," *Los Angeles Times*, January 25, 1989, p. 7.

25. Scott Armstrong, "Los Angeles Confronts More Youth Violence," *Christian Science Monitor*, February 24, 1988, p. 3.

26. Vrcan.

27. Klein and Maxson, p. 227.

28. Ibid.

29. Ibid., pp. 226–29.

Chapter Thirteen: Sexual Violence

1. Anastasia Toufexis, "Teenagers and Sex Crimes," *Time*, June 5, 1989, p. 60.

2. Gilda Berger, *Violence in the Family* (New York: Franklin Watts, 1990), p. 95.

3. Toufexis, "Teenagers."
4. Ronald Lauder, *Fighting Violent Crime in America* (New York: Dodd, Mead, 1985), p. 72.
5. "Teens and Crime Prevention," *Children Today*, March–April 1988, p. 2.
6. Jean Seligmann, "The Date Who Rapes," *Newsweek*, April 9, 1984, p. 91.
7. John Leo, "When the Date Turns into Rape," *Time*, March 23, 1987, p. 77.
8. Mark Eyerly, "Date Rape Now Subject of a Book by Andrea Parrot," *Cornell Chronicle*, May 19, 1988, p. 4.
9. Seligmann, p. 91.
10. Berger, *Violence in the Family*, p. 92; and Bonnie E. Carlson, "Dating Violence," *Social-Casework*, January 1987, vol. 68, no. 1, pp. 16–23.
11. Ibid., p. 93.
12. Susan Lang, " 'Date Rape' Is a Hidden Epidemic," *Ithaca Journal*, December 30, 1985, p. 10
13. Toufexis, "Teenagers," p. 50.
14. "What's Happening to Our Youth: Central Park Tragedy and Glen Ridge Attack," "Donahue," May 31, 1989, show #53189, television broadcast on NBC.
15. Toufexis, "Teenagers."

Chapter Fourteen: Kids Who Kill . . . Themselves

1. From cartoon by Higgins, 1987 *Chicago Sun Times,* in Sandra R. Arbetter, MSW, "By Their Own Hands," *Current Health*, September 1987, p. 18.
2. Jack Frymer, "Understanding and Preventing Teen Suicide," *Phi Delta Kappa,* December 1988, p. 290.
3. Mary Griffin, M.D., *A Cry for Help* (Garden City, N.Y.: Doubleday, 1983), p. 5.
4. "Teen Suicide and Handguns" (Washington, D.C.: Center to Prevent Handgun Violence, April 1989).
5. Centers for Disease Control, *Youth Suicide Surveillance, 1986,* Johns Hopkins University, School of Hygiene and Public Health, in "Teen Suicide and Handguns."
6. Ibid.
7. *National Adolescent Student Health Survey, 1988,* U.S. Department of Health and Human Services, in "Teen Suicide and Handguns."
8. Lucy Davidson, Mark Rosenberg, et al., "An Epidemiologic Study of Risk Factors in Two Teenage Suicide Clusters," *The Journal of the American Medical Association,* November 17, 1989, p. 2687.
9. B. H. Balser and J. F. Masterson, "Suicide in Adolescents," *American Journal of Psychiatry* 116 (1959): pp. 400–04, in Pamela Cantor, "Suicide and Depression: 'Too Sad to Live,' " Action for Children's Television, *TV and Teens: Experts Look at the Issues* (Reading, Mass.: Addison Wesley, 1982), p. 177.
10. Frymer.
11. Gilda Berger, *Violence and the Media* (New York: Franklin Watts, 1989), p. 37.

12. Frymer.
13. Amy Wilentz, "Teen Suicide," *Time*, March 23, 1987, p. 12.
14. "Workshop, Suicide," in Annette Zimmern Reed, Ph.D., ed., *Violence in America* (Austin, Tex.: Family Advocacy Program, U.S. Air Force 1986), p. 161.

Chapter Fifteen: What Can Be Done?
 1. George Miller, "Give Kids an Option Besides Gang Life," *Los Angeles Times*, April 10, 1988, Section 5, p. 5.
 2. Daniel Goleman, "Taming Unruly Boys: Old Techniques and New Approaches," *New York Times*, February 1, 1990, p. B10.
 3. Norma Deitch Feshback, "Empathy, Empathy Training, and the Regulation of Aggression in Elementary School Children," in Robert Kaplan, ed., *Aggression in Children and Youth* (Boston: Martinus Nijhoff Publishers, 1984), pp. 192–208.
 4. Robert S. Clark, *Deadly Force: The Lure of Violence* (Springfield, Ill.: Charles C. Thomas, 1988), pp. 221–237.
 5. Daniel B. Wood, "From Street to Stage, Gang Becomes a Troupe," *Christian Science Monitor*, June 28, 1988, p. 1.
 6. Miller.
 7. Mortimer Zuckerman, "Meltdown in Our Cities," *U.S. News & World Report*, May 29, 1989, p. 74.
 8. Clifford Krauss, "Reacting to Crimes, Police Plan to Pick Up Truants," *New York Times*, February 24, 1994, p. 1.
 9. Susan Tifft, "Fighting the Failure Syndrome," *Time*, May 21, 1990.
10. "Teens and Crime Prevention," *Children Today*, March–April 1988, p. 2.
11. Ronald S. Lauder, *Fighting Violent Crime in America* (New York: Dodd, Mead, 1985), p. 103.
12. Tom Post, "Farewell to Arms," *Newsweek*, January 10, 1994, p. 21.
13. Clifford Krauss, "Giuliani Plans Initiative to Curb Gun Violence," *New York Times*, February 27, 1994, p. 31.
14. Mortimer Zuckerman, "War on Crime, By the Numbers," *U.S. News & World Report*, January 17, 1994, p. 68.
15. Michael Barone, "Time to Shatter the Crime Culture," *U.S. News & World Report*, January 17, 1994, p. 42.
16. William Sanders, *Juvenile Delinquency: Causes, Patterns, and Reactions* (New York: Holt, Rinehart and Winston) 1981.
17. "Study Shows Restitution is Best Solution to Juvenile Crime," Arizona State University news release, July 29, 1990.
18. Rita Kramer, *At a Tender Age: Violent Youth and Juvenile Justice* (New York: Henry Holt & Co., 1988), p. 251.
19. Alex Kotlowitz, "Their Crimes Don't Make Them Adults," *New York Times Magazine*, February 13, 1994, p. 40.
20. Jeff Coplon, "Young, Bad, & Dangerous," *Ladies' Home Journal*, August 1985, p. 166.
21. "Ex-Offenders Aid World of Disabled," *New York Times*, February 4, 1990, p. 34.
22. Miller.

FOR FURTHER READING

American Psychological Association, Violence and Youth Division. *Psychology's Response*. Washington, D.C.: APA, 1993.

Baker, Falcon. *Saving Our Kids From Delinquency, Drugs and Despair: Solutions Through Prevention*. New York: Cornelia and Michael Bessie Books, 1991.

Bartollas, Clemens. *Juvenile Delinquency*. New York: John Wiley, 1985.

Berger, Gilda. *Violence and Drugs*. New York: Franklin Watts, 1989.

——*Violence and the Family*. New York: Franklin Watts, 1990.

——*Violence and the Media*. New York: Franklin Watts, 1989.

Carlsson-Paige, Nancy, and Levin, Diane. *Who's Calling the Shots?: How to Respond Effectively to Children's Fascination with War Play and War Toys*. Philadelphia: New Society Publishers, 1990.

Clark, Robert S., Ph.D. *The Lure of Deadly Force*. Springfield, Ill.: Charles C. Thomas, 1988.

Cromwell, David H.; Evans, Ian M.; and O'Donnell, Clifford R., eds. *Childhood Aggression and Violence: Sources of Influence, Prevention, and Control*. New York: Plenum Press, 1987.

Ewing, Charles Patrick. *Kids Who Kill*. New York, Lexington Books, 1990.

Giovacchini, Peter, M.D. *The Urge to Die: Why Young People Commit Suicide*. New York: Macmillan, 1981.

Gordon, Sol. *When Living Hurts*. New York: Union of American Hebrew Congregations, 1985.

Griffin, Mary, M.S., and Carol Felsenthal. *A Cry for Help*. New York: Doubleday, 1983.

Hansen, Gladys. *Violence in the Sandbox: A Guide for Children, Parents, Preschool and Teachers*. Los Angeles: Little Children Productions, 1982.

Juvenile Justice Clearinghouse. *Violent Offenders: An Anthology*, NCJ 995108. Pepperdine University, Box 6000, Rockville, MD 20850. (Helps schools respond to gangs, drugs, and violence by providing technical help, training, and resource materials to rid schools of crime, violence, and drugs and to improve discipline, attendance, student achievement, and the learning environment.)

Kaplan, Robert M.; Konecni, Vladimir J.; and Raymond W. Novaco, eds. *Aggression in Children and Youth*. Boston: Martinus Nijhoff Publishers, 1984.

Lang, Susan. *Extremist Groups in America*. New York: Franklin Watts, 1990.

Lefkowitz, Monroe M. et al. *Growing Up to Be Violent: A Longitudinal Study of the Development of Aggression*. New York: Pergamon Press, 1977.

Prothrow-Stith, Deborah, M.D. and Michaele Weissman. *Deadly Consequences: How Violence is Destroying Our Teenage Population and a Plan to Begin Solving the Problem*. New York: HarperCollins, 1991.

Reed, Annette Zimmern, Ph.D. *Violence in America: Proceedings of the Southwest Regional Research Conference, November 6–8, 1986*. Austin,

Tex.: U.S. Air Force Family Advocacy Program, 1987.

Rojek, Dean G., and Jensen, Gary F. *Readings in Juvenile Delinquency*. Lexington, Mass.: D.C. Heath, 1982.

Rutter, Michael, and Giller, Henri. *Juvenile Delinquency: Trends and Perspectives*. New York: Guilford Press, 1984.

Sandburg, David N. *The Child Abuse-Delinquency Connection*. Lexington, Mass.: Lexington Books, D.C. Heath, 1989.

Sanders, William B. *Juvenile Delinquency: Causes, Patterns, and Reactions*. New York: Holt, Rinehart and Winston, 1981.

Schwendinger, Herman, and Schwendinger, Julia Siegel. *Adolescent Subcultures and Delinquency*. New York: Praeger, 1985.

Showmaker, Donald J. *Theories of Delinquency: An Examination of Explanations of Delinquent Behavior*. New York: Oxford University Press, 1982.

Stanton, Samenow. *Before It's Too Late: Why Some Kids Get Into Trouble & What Parents Can Do About It*. New York: Times Books, 1989.

Taylor, Carl. *Dangerous Society*. Lansing: Michigan State University Press, 1990.

Weiner, Neil Alan, and Wolfgang, Marvin E., eds. *Pathways to Criminal Violence*. Newbury Park, Calif.: Sage Publications, 1989.

———*Violent Crime, Violent Criminals*. Newbury Park, Calif.: Sage Publications, 1989.

Wolfgang, Marvin. *The Subculture of Violence*. Beverly Hills, Calif.: Sage Publications, 1982.

Wolfgang, Marvin E., Thornberry, Terence P.; and Figlio, Robert M. *From Boy to Man: From Delinquency to Crime*. University of Chicago Press, 1987.

Zevin, Jack. *Violence in America: What Is the Alternative?* Englewood Cliffs, N.J.: Prentice-Hall, 1973.

INDEX